Beyond the Screen and Page:
Sci-Fi Stories in Verse

Brandon Michaels

Beyond the Screen and Page:
Sci-Fi Stories in Verse
All Rights Reserved

𝕏

@AuthorBMichaels

www.authorbrandonmichaels.com

www.nudouspublishing.com
info@nudouspublishing.com

Paperback ISBN: 978-1-964793-90-0

Dedication

Thank you to the extraordinary science fiction writers who have expanded our horizons and challenged us to see the universe—and ourselves—in entirely new ways. Your creativity and imagination have given us worlds to explore, questions to ponder, and futures to dream about. You have shown us that the impossible can become possible and that curiosity and innovation are the keys to progress.

Your stories have been a source of wonder, inspiration, and endless fascination. This book exists because of the foundation you've built and the paths you've paved. Thank you for your vision and for daring to take us where no one has gone before.

1/20/2025

Dear Readers,

Thank you for picking up this book and joining me on a journey through the vast and imaginative universe of science fiction. Your support means the world to me, and I'm thrilled to share this collection of poems with you.

As a lifelong lover of science fiction, I've always been inspired by incredible worlds, thought-provoking ideas, and unforgettable characters created by some of the greatest storytellers. These poems are my humble tribute to the shows, movies, and books that have sparked my imagination, challenged my perspectives, and reminded me of the boundless possibilities that lie beyond the stars.

Each piece in this collection reflects my deep admiration for the genre and the creators who dared to dream boldly. Whether it's the futuristic landscapes, the moral dilemmas, or the awe-inspiring adventures, science fiction has a unique ability to transport us to new dimensions while holding up a mirror to our humanity.

I hope these poems resonate with you, whether they remind you of your favorite stories or introduce you to new ones. Most importantly, I hope they capture even a small fraction of the wonder and inspiration that science fiction has given to me.

Warm regards,
Brandon Michaels

Table of Contents

Ballad of the Serenity Crew

Beneath the stars so wide and free,

A ship named *Serenity* sails the sea.

Her rusted hull and battered grace,

A rebel's home, a wild embrace.

Malcolm leads with a soldier's pride,

A captain torn by wars denied.

In shadows deep, his heart still aches,

For freedom lost and the past it takes.

Zoe stands tall, her courage pure,

A warrior's strength, steadfast and sure.

By her side, Wash flies the skies,

With wit that sparkles and love that ties.

Kaylee hums with a spanner's song,

Fixing the broken, where others go wrong.

Her hands bring life, her smile brings light,

A beacon in the darkest night.

Jayne, the muscle, with morals thin,

A mercenary with a grin of sin.

Yet deep within, a heart may beat,

Buried beneath his deeds' deceit.

River dances, her mind askew,

A puzzle of genius, a tortured view.

Simon stays, her steadfast shield,

To protect the sister fate has reeled.

Inara glides with a courtesan's art,

Graceful and poised, yet guarding her heart.

A tether of tension, a love unspoken,

In silence held, but never broken.

Book, the Shepherd, with secrets to bear,

A past concealed in a preacher's prayer.

Guidance given, his wisdom true,

A path of peace for the wandering crew.

Through worlds uncharted, dangers vast,

They find their bonds will always last.

For in the black, where stars don't shine,

The crew of *Serenity* draw the line.

A firefly's glow in the endless night,

A spark of hope, a fleeting light.

Though stories end, the spirit remains,

The *Serenity* soars through memory's plains.

Through the Gate: A Stargate SG-1 Ode

A ring of stone, with glyphs aglow,
An ancient key to worlds unknown.
The Stargate hums, its secrets vast,
A journey through the distant past.

Colonel O'Neill, with wit so dry,
A soldier's resolve, a skeptic's eye.
He leads the charge, the fearless guide,
With humor sharp and courage wide.

Dr. Jackson, the scholar, seeks,
In ancient tongues, the truth he speaks.
Through myths and lore, he finds the way,
To light the dark and save the day.

Carter, the genius, her brilliance shines,
Her mind a map of quantum lines.
She solves the riddles, breaks the code,
A scientist's heart, a warrior's mode.

Teal'c, the Jaffa, with honor bound,
A rebel's strength, his wisdom profound.
With staff in hand and stoic might,
He fights for freedom, for what is right.

Through desert sands and icy plains,

Through forests deep and cosmic chains,

They face the Goa'uld, their ruthless foes,

And challenge all the power they pose.

The Asgard aid with a guiding hand,

While Ancients' secrets shift like sand.

The team endures through trials dire,

With hope that burns like a cosmic fire.

The Stargate spins, the wormhole swirls,

To alien worlds with flags unfurled.

Each mission brings a chance to see,

The boundless scope of destiny.

So raise a toast to SG-1,

For battles fought and victories won.

Through space and time, their story's told,

A legacy of courage bold.

City Beneath the Waves: A Stargate Atlantis Poem

Beneath the sea, in a galaxy far,
Lies Atlantis, the Ancients' star.
A city of wonder, a beacon of light,
Lost in the depths, shrouded in night.

The Stargate spins, the team arrives,
A journey bold to save their lives.
With courage strong and hopes held high,
They seek new worlds beyond the sky.

Dr. Weir, with wisdom's grace,
Leads the charge in this alien place.
Her voice of reason, calm and clear,
Guides the crew through doubt and fear.

Sheppard stands, a soldier's pride,
With reckless charm as his faithful guide.
A leader born, though rough around,
In him, a loyal heart is found.

McKay, the genius, sharp and brash,
His mind a blaze, his tongue a lash.
Yet in his quirks, a hero's might,
To solve the puzzle, to win the fight.

Teyla, the warrior, with wisdom's calm,
Her people's strength, her spirit's balm.
With staff in hand and heart so true,
She fights for peace for all they knew.

Ronon, the hunter, with scars so deep,
A past of loss, where shadows creep.
His loyalty fierce, his blade a shield,
On every front, he takes the field.

The Wraith emerge, a deadly foe,
Feeding on life's energy flow.
Through battles fierce and dangers vast,
The team fights on, their shadows cast.

Through ancient halls and distant stars,
They seek the truth of who we are.
A city's secrets, a galaxy's plight,
Explored in courage, love, and light.

Atlantis shines beneath the waves,
A testament to the brave who save.
Though journeys end and tales must fade,
Its legacy lives, forever made.

The Expanse: A Ballad of the Void

In the vast and silent ocean wide,
Where planets turn and secrets hide,
The Belt and Earth, and Mars divide,
A fragile peace the stars provide.

The Canterbury, a freighter's fate,
A spark ignites, a war innate.
From icy rings to darkened skies,
The truth unfolds through countless lies.

James Holden, with a captain's gaze,
Seeks justice through the cosmos' maze.
A crew of outcasts, bound by trust,
Their ship *Rocinante*, forged from dust.

Naomi, the Belter, with knowledge vast,
Her wisdom guides through shadows cast.
A heart that beats for those who roam,
She finds her strength so far from home.

Amos, the muscle, with a haunted past,
A soldier's grit that holds steadfast.
Beneath the steel, a loyal core,
A shield for friends when threats outpour.

Alex, the pilot, with Martian pride,

Through cosmic storms, he's always tried.

His skillful hands, the ship's own wings,

To navigate where danger sings.

Through Eros' depths and Venus' glow,

The Protomolecule's tendrils grow.

A mystery ancient, a force untamed,

A power that none have fully named.

Avasarala, with a diplomat's fire,

Wields her words to shape the empire.

Her cunning mind, a weapon keen,

In courts of power, she reigns unseen.

The Belt, in struggle, cries for breath,

A life oppressed, a fate near death.

Their fight for freedom, a rebel's plea,

A voice that echoes eternity.

The Expanse unfolds, a tale of might,

Of human greed and cosmic light.

Through stars and void, the battle's fought,

For peace and hope, for all that's sought.

Though borders bind and powers vie,

The spirit of unity will not die.

For in the dark where stars ignite,

Humanity endures the endless night.

The 100: A Song of Survival

A hundred souls to Earth they send,
To test if life might bloom again.
The Ark above, its time run out,
A fragile hope, a desperate shout.

Clarke, the leader, with wisdom torn,
Bears every burden the young have borne.
Her heart and mind, a steady flame,
Through loss and pain, she earns her name.

Bellamy fights with a brother's care,
His strength a shield, his heart laid bare.
A soldier's grit, a rebel's fire,
He finds his path through mud and mire.

Octavia, the girl who rose from ash,
Her blade as swift as a lightning flash.
From "Sky Girl" to the warrior's queen,
Her journey fierce, her soul between.

Raven's mind, a forge of steel,
With tools in hand, she bends and heals.
A genius bound by scars and strain,
Her courage forged in fire and pain.

Murphy, the rogue, a survivor's wit,

Through shadows dark, he won't submit.

A heart once hardened, slowly thawed,

Redeemed by bonds that once seemed flawed.

The Grounders' ways, the clans they fight,

Their war cries pierce the starless night.

A culture deep, with honor bound,

Their bloodied hands defend their ground.

The Mountain men, with terror's hand,

Brought poison air to Earth's fair land.

Their hunger cruel, their actions dire,

Consumed by greed, they lit the pyre.

The City of Light, a false reprieve,

A digital dream meant to deceive.

Through war and chaos, the truth they find,

That peace is won through heart and mind.

Through flames and loss, through war's cruel strife,

They cling to hope, to love, to life.

For even when the skies turn black,

They fight to bring their people back.

The hundred rise, though worlds may break,

Their will endures for the future's sake.

In Earth's embrace or stars above,

Their story burns with strength and love.

Beyond the Outer Limits

There is a door, a threshold wide,
Where the known and unknown collide.
A realm of wonder, fear, and might,
A journey deep into the night.

"Do not adjust," the voice intones,
"This boundary lies within your bones."
A twist of fate, a truth unclear,
A tale of what we hold most dear.

The cosmos vast, a mirror's face,
Reflects the dreams of the human race.
Through science bent and morals tried,
We face ourselves with nowhere to hide.

A man with power, his mind untamed,
Creates a world where none are blamed.
But greed and hubris bear their cost,
A paradise built, forever lost.

A child's gaze turns stars to flame,
A universe shaped by a simple name.
What horrors lie in innocence vast,
When wielded by hands too small to grasp?

The alien calls, the unknown speaks,

Through whispered truths and haunting peaks.

A test of will, of fear's embrace,

To find our place in time and space.

Machines awaken, their hearts of steel,

Echo the lives they've learned to feel.

Their logic pure, their actions strange,

A question lingers: can we change?

Through distant stars or minds within,

Each story turns on mortal sin.

The Outer Limits shows the line,

Between what's human and divine.

So dare to dream, but tread with care,

For what you find may leave you bare.

A haunting truth, a world unmade,

A glimpse of shadows we ourselves have laid.

For in this realm of dark and light,

We test the soul, the depth of sight.

Beyond the limits, a voice persists:

"The answer lies where fear exists."

A Journey to the Twilight Zone

You unlock this door with a curious key,
To a world beyond what the eye can see.
A realm of shadow, a space unknown,
Welcome, traveler, to the Twilight Zone.

A clock that ticks, but time won't flow,
A mirror's face that doesn't show.
The ordinary twists, the mundane bends,
Reality's thread frays and ends.

A man alone, his books his prize,
Yet the world dissolves before his eyes.
Time to read, but at what cost?
The fragile line of hope is lost.

A diner's jukebox, a fortune's phrase,
Predicts the fate of coming days.
But is it chance, or something more?
A cosmic game behind the door.

A boy who smiles, but all must heed,
For his thoughts become the world indeed.
In fear, they praise his every whim,
A child-god's rule, both bright and grim.

A flight through storms, a gremlin's leer,

A haunted wing, a pilot's fear.

Do monsters dwell in the open skies,

Or in the depths of a fractured mind?

The small-town man who casts no shade,

A bargain struck, a devil's trade.

For riches vast or power's might,

What part of soul would you ignite?

Each episode, a mirror's frame,

Reflecting truths we fear to name.

Our follies, fears, and dreams untamed,

In twilight's glow, all are proclaimed.

Rod Serling's voice, a guide so clear,

Draws you close, yet whispers near:

"Step carefully where shadows roam,

For you've now entered the Twilight Zone."

A twist of fate, a chilling hue,

A glimpse of worlds both old and new.

In black and white, the stories gleam,

Where nothing's ever as it seems.

A Martian's Soliloquy

Alone beneath a crimson sky,

Where dust and silence never die,

A stranded man, with wit and will,

Turns barren Mars to fertile thrill.

Mark Watney, cast from Earth's embrace,

Fights for life in an alien place.

With science sharp and humor keen,

He bends the red to hues of green.

A patchwork farm, a soil reborn,

From Earth's own seed, potatoes are sworn.

Each sprout a hope, each root a prayer,

For sustenance in the Martian air.

The Hab, his fortress, fragile yet,

A home he builds where none is set.

With duct tape, code, and stubborn grit,

He fashions life where death had writ.

The rover hums, his lifeline true,

Across the wasteland's endless view.

From Ares' path to Pathfinder's grace,

He reaches out through time and space.

On Earth, they see his silent plea,

A castaway for the world to see.

The nations rise, their borders blur,

For one man's life, they all confer.

A daring crew, their course they change,

To save their friend through risks most strange.

Their bond defies the void's expanse,

A testament to the human chance.

Through every trial, every test,

Watney laughs, survives, and rests.

His tale a spark, a beacon's flame,

That whispers softly: "Play the game."

For even when the odds are dire,

The human heart burns like a fire.

On Mars's red, in cold, stark hue,

He proves what courage can renew.

So here's to Mark, to hope, to strife,

To science wielded to foster life.

A lone man's fight, a world's shared cheer,

The Martian's tale, Andy Weir.

The OASIS Awaits: A Poem for *Ready Player One*

A world in ruins, bleak and gray,
Where skies of sorrow cloud the day.
But through the code, a door is found,
To realms where dreams and hope abound.

The OASIS gleams, a vast domain,
A digital life to escape the pain.
From endless quests to battles grand,
A universe shaped by a gamer's hand.

Parzival strides, a name of might,
In virtual halls of neon light.
Wade Watts beneath, a life so bare,
Yet in the game, he's free to dare.

Anorak's Hunt, the challenge set,
By Halliday, a riddle yet unmet.
Three keys, three gates, the prize untold,
A fortune vast, a crown of gold.

Art3mis stands, a rival and muse,
Her brilliance sharp, her courage true.
With wit as keen as her digital blade,
She joins the fight where legends are made.

Aech, the friend, a steady guide,

With secrets hidden deep inside.

A bond of trust, a brother's cheer,

Through trials faced, they persevere.

The Sixers rise, with greed their creed,

To claim the throne, to feed their need.

Corporate might, a soulless quest,

Against their power, the players contest.

Through '80s lore and pixel streams,

Through vivid worlds and fleeting dreams,

The gunters race to crack the code,

To claim the path that Halliday showed.

The battle fought, the victory earned,

A lesson deep from quests well-learned:

That friendship, love, and a heart sincere,

Are treasures vast, beyond the sphere.

So here's to Wade, to dreams reborn,

To worlds of wonder where none are torn.

In Ernest Cline's electrified tone,

We find our place in the unknown.

Chronicles of the Merry Band: An *Expeditionary Force Poem*

From Earth's blue skies to the stars' cold glow,
A tale of courage begins to grow.
Joe Bishop, a soldier's name,
Pulled from Earth to join the game.

An alien war, humanity's plight,
A fragile world caught in the fight.
Yet through the chaos, a bond takes root,
Between a man and an AI's pursuit.

Skippy the Magnificent, a can of sass,
A being of knowledge, with humor to surpass.
With snarky wit and logic keen,
He's more than a sidekick; he's the scene.

The Merry Band, a ragtag crew,
Faces odds that would break the few.
Through space and time, they twist and turn,
In every scrape, new lessons learned.

The Ruhar clash with the Kristang's might,
A battle raging, wrong and right.
Yet beneath the war's chaotic veil,
Lies secrets vast, a deeper tale.

Joe and Skippy, an unlikely pair,

Outsmart the foes with cunning flair.

From wormhole leaps to battles fierce,

Their bond grows strong, their mission pierce.

Through stealthy runs and plans gone wrong,

Their victories hum with a chaotic song.

The banter flies, the stakes grow steep,

As galaxy-spanning secrets they keep.

The universe vast, its dangers near,

Yet friendship triumphs over fear.

For even when the path seems dire,

The Merry Band will not retire.

So here's to Joe, to Skippy's might,

To a tale that shines like a starry night.

Craig Alanson's world, a thrilling spree,

A saga of wit, and a destiny free.

Frontlines: A Soldier's Tale

From Earth's worn soil to the stars above,
A story of war, loss, and love.
In ranks they march, through fire and rain,
Humanity's fight, both hope and pain.

Andrew Grayson, a name unsung,
A soldier's life, his journey begun.
From poverty's grip to the fleet's embrace,
He seeks a future in endless space.

The Lankies loom, a towering threat,
Their motives cold, their hearts unset.
Through ships and stars, they claim their ground,
A silent force, their steps resound.

With rifle in hand, through blood and grit,
Grayson fights where the brave commit.
Each battle fought, a test of will,
Against the void that seeks to kill.

Earth's cradle strains beneath the weight,
Of wars that shape a fragile fate.
From colony worlds to cosmic black,
The Frontlines hold, no turning back.

Chandra stands, a partner and peer,

A bond that grows in moments severe.

Together they face the chaos ahead,

In love and war, where paths are led.

The chain of command, both curse and guide,

A soldier's burden they cannot hide.

Through loyalty torn and orders grim,

They fight for all, though chances slim.

Through orbital drops and frozen ground,

Through Lanky skies and their hallowed sound,

The human spirit endures the fight,

A fragile flame in the endless night.

Marko Kloos pens the soldier's plight,

A tale of courage, dark and bright.

For on the Frontlines, hearts are tried,

In a galaxy vast, where heroes stride.

For All Mankind: A Poetic Journey

The moon, a beacon in the night,

A stage for dreams, a field for flight.

In alternate paths, the story bends,

Where history shifts and vision extends.

The Eagle lands, yet not alone,

A Soviet flag beside our own.

The race renewed, the stakes redrawn,

As nations vie beneath the dawn.

Ed Baldwin, a pilot's pride,

With scars of loss and strength inside.

Through trials deep, his spirit soars,

In cosmic realms, on distant shores.

Danielle fights with steadfast grace,

Breaking barriers in space's embrace.

Her courage shines, her voice so clear,

A pioneer who knows no fear.

Margo steers with a mind so keen,

Her brilliance fuels the NASA dream.

Yet secrets weigh her fragile heart,

A scientist torn, her truths apart.

Gordo and Tracy, a tangled thread,

Love and loss in paths they tread.

Through laughter, pain, and sacrifice,

Their legacies burn through coldest ice.

The sea of stars, a stage so vast,

For human hope to outlast.

Mars, the prize, a new frontier,

A testament to what we hold dear.

But in the void, ambition grows,

And power's shadow always shows.

For every step, a cost is paid,

In lives and dreams, foundations laid.

The Cold War's chill, the cosmos wide,

A fragile peace, a swelling tide.

Through fire and failure, the dream persists,

To touch the stars with clenched fists.

A vision bold, a story grand,

Of courage born in humankind's hand.

"For All Mankind," a tale retold,

Of futures shaped by hearts so bold.

Legacy Fleet: A Starfighter's Song

The Earth grows old, her fleets outdated,

A peace once earned, but now ill-fated.

The Swarm returns, a shadow vast,

A terror reborn from the echoes of past.

Admiral Granger, a name revered,

A leader forged in times so seared.

With duty bound and courage steeled,

He takes the helm on the battlefield.

The *Concordia*, a ship of lore,

A relic now, yet so much more.

Its battered hull, its engines hum,

A symbol strong of battles won.

The Swarm descends, relentless tide,

Through voids uncharted, no place to hide.

Their silence speaks, their fury roars,

As humanity braces for galactic wars.

Pilots rise, their hearts aflame,

To defend their worlds in the deadly game.

Through dogfights fierce and cosmic strife,

They gamble stars with their very life.

Blackwood stands, her spirit fierce,

With every loss, her soul is pierced.

A fighter's heart, her will unbowed,

In every battle, she makes us proud.

Science blends with courage raw,

Old ships enhanced to defy the law.

For in the cracks of time's decay,

A legacy fights to light the way.

Through alien fleets and desperate calls,

Through heroes' rise and empires' falls,

The Legacy Fleet endures the fight,

A beacon bright in the endless night.

Nick Webb pens a future dire,

Of wars that test and hearts that inspire.

For in the stars, humanity thrives,

A testament to how hope survives.

The Fragile Chain: A Poem for *The Interdependency*

A galaxy bound by a thread unseen,
The Flow connects where worlds convene.
A fragile chain, a lifeline clear,
Yet whispers tell of its end near.

The Emperox rises, unprepared,
Cardenia Wu-Patrick, a ruler ensnared.
Thrust to power, her crown a weight,
To guide her people through uncertain fate.

The Interdependency thrives on trade,
A web of worlds, alliances made.
Yet cracks appear as the Flow declines,
A universe trembling at collapsing lines.

Marce Claremont, the scholar keen,
Sees truths within the data's sheen.
A scientist's voice in the chaos loud,
A herald of doom through the panicked crowd.

Kiva Lagos, with wit so sharp,
A merchant bold with a cunning heart.
Her schemes and strength, her fearless fire,
A force unyielding in stakes so dire.

The Nohamapetan's ruthless play,

A family bent on power's sway.

Their treachery burns, their greed unfolds,

In the shadow of collapse, their grasp takes hold.

Worlds grow restless, alliances strain,

As Flow streams vanish, chaos reigns.

Through politics fierce and battles dire,

The Emperox lights a beacon's fire.

In John Scalzi's tale of wit and might,

A future struggles for its light.

The Interdependency stands or falls,

A story of hope as the darkness calls.

For even as the Flow may fade,

And systems die where life was made,

The human spirit dares to fight,

To forge a path in the endless night.

Seveneves: A Poem of the End and Beginning

The moon is torn, its pieces stray,

A harbinger of Earth's last day.

Humanity looks to the skies in dread,

As fiery fragments herald the dead.

Seven years, the countdown tolls,

To save a world, to save our souls.

The Ark, a hope in orbit's span,

A fragile dream for the race of man.

Dinah soars with her robotic kin,

Mining space to fight within.

A tinkerer's mind, a heart of steel,

Her courage bends the cosmos' wheel.

Ivy commands with steady hand,

A leader bound to a fractured band.

Through chaos vast, her strength inspires,

A beacon bright in falling empires.

Tekla guards with unyielding might,

A soldier forged in endless night.

Her loyalty fierce, her presence bold,

A warrior's tale in legends told.

The Hard Rain falls, the Earth undone,

A fiery wrath eclipses the sun.

The skies ablaze, the surface dies,

While life persists where hope still flies.

Seven Eves, a lineage sown,

Each shaping futures yet unknown.

Genetic threads, humanity's spark,

Rewoven now from the void's dark.

Millennia pass, a world reborn,

A patchwork sky, a scattered morn.

The Cloud Ark's children reach for stars,

To mend the wounds of ancient scars.

Neal Stephenson weaves a tale profound,

Of ends and starts, where hope is found.

For even as the Earth may sever,

The human spirit endures forever.

Locked In: A Poem for the Haden's World

A virus strikes, unseen, unknown,
Through the world its shadow's thrown.
A silent thief, it takes the voice,
And leaves its victims with no choice.

Haden's Syndrome, the name it bears,
A life encased in frozen stares.
Locked in bodies, minds still bright,
Seeking freedom in the night.

The Agora blooms, a digital space,
Where Hadens gather, mind's embrace.
Through streams of code, they learn to fly,
Beyond the limits of the eye.

Integrators walk where Hadens can't,
Sharing bodies, a living grant.
Yet in this merging, a price is paid,
For blurred lines made in the life they trade.

Chris Shane, a Haden, stands apart,
An FBI agent with a driven heart.
With wit and grit, they seek the truth,
Through webs of lies, through crime's dark roots.

A partner strong, Detective Vann,

Her past a shadow, her will a span.

Together they face the world askew,

Where justice calls and dangers brew.

Murder, greed, and schemes unfold,

A future fraught with stories untold.

Yet through it all, a question looms,

Of what it means in these locked rooms.

John Scalzi's pen brings light to bear,

On lives reshaped by trials rare.

For even locked within, they strive,

To show the world they're still alive.

A tale of hope, of courage vast,

Of bonds that form and truths that last.

Through bodies still and minds unchained,

The human spirit is retained.

Project Hail Mary: A Starborne Prayer

Alone he wakes, his mind a haze,

A silent ship, a sunlit gaze.

Ryland Grace, with no recall,

Finds himself on a cosmic call.

The mission clear, the stakes immense,

A dying Earth, its last defense.

Astrophage drains the starry light,

And threatens all with endless night.

Through science, wit, and daring feats,

Grace pieces clues where answers meet.

His mind a forge, his heart unsure,

A teacher thrust to the hero's cure.

Then from the void, a sound, a plea,

A voice that echoes, alien, free.

Rocky appears, a friend profound,

A being of strength where hope is found.

Their languages clash, their worlds divide,

Yet trust and humor bridge the tide.

Together they face the deadly race,

To bring salvation to each one's place.

Through engines hum and starlit skies,

They venture where no answer lies.

A bond is formed, unspoken, deep,

A friendship carved where stars still sleep.

The challenges rise, the risks increase,

But Grace persists for Earth's release.

For in his hands, a future gleams,

A fragile thread of human dreams.

Andy Weir pens this thrilling tale,

Of problem-solving beyond the pale.

A hymn to science, to hearts that try,

A prayer that echoes through the sky.

So here's to hope, to bonds that last,

To saving worlds, to learning fast.

Through stardust vast and trials grim,

The light of Earth begins to dim—

But never fades, for we endure,

A species striving to find its cure.

Artemis: A Lunar Song

Beneath the Moon's eternal glow,
A city thrives where few dare go.
Artemis stands, a beacon bright,
In lunar dust and endless night.

Jasmine Bashara, Jazz by name,
A dreamer bold in the smuggler's game.
With wit as sharp as her ambitions soar,
She walks the line on Artemis's floor.

A porter's life, a hustler's creed,
She bends the rules to serve her need.
Yet fate conspires, a dangerous task,
A job too big, too much to ask.

Trond's offer, a chance so grand,
To shift the balance of lunar land.
Sabotage and secrets unfold,
In a city of silver, corruption cold.

Through domes of glass and corridors tight,
Jazz races on through the lunar night.
With every step, her courage grows,
As danger lurks and truth bestows.

Friends and foes, their motives blend,

Allies shift as plots extend.

Svoboda's quirks and Dale's disdain,

Jazz navigates through loss and gain.

Oxygen's scarce, betrayal's rife,

The cost of freedom: her very life.

Yet Jazz persists, her spirit burns,

Through trials vast, her fortune turns.

Andy Weir crafts a tale profound,

Where science and cunning tightly bound.

A heroine flawed, yet fierce and strong,

In Artemis, she rights the wrong.

So toast the Moon, to dreams that fly,

To those who thrive beneath its sky.

In lunar dust, the bold remain,

Their grit and hope the brightest flame.

Babylon 5: A Beacon in the Stars

In endless black, where shadows creep,
A station stands, a vigil to keep.
Babylon 5, a dream of peace,
A fragile hope that wars may cease.

The year is marked, the tensions rise,
A battleground beneath the skies.
Nations clash, alliances fray,
Yet light endures in the dimmest day.

Sinclair begins with a leader's grace,
A steady hand in a volatile space.
Sheridan follows, with fire and will,
A soldier's heart, a strategist's skill.

Delenn, the bridge of old and new,
With wisdom deep and vision true.
Minbari grace and human heart,
She weaves the threads of worlds apart.

G'Kar, the Narn, with fury born,
Seeks justice where his race was torn.
Through pain and loss, his spirit grows,
A path of wisdom his life bestows.

Londo dreams of glory's reign,

Yet finds himself in shadow's chain.

The Centauri's fall, a price too steep,

For power's grasp and promises to keep.

Vir, the quiet, the conscience clear,

A voice of hope when none appear.

In darkness vast, his kindness shines,

A star that guides through cruel designs.

The Vorlons speak in cryptic tones,

Their motives shrouded, their truths unknown.

The Shadows rise, their chaos spreads,

In ancient wars, the future treads.

Through battles fierce and secrets told,

Through love and loss, the brave uphold.

The Line is drawn, the stakes are high,

As empires burn and heroes die.

J. Michael Straczynski's pen inspires,

A tale of stars and heart's desires.

For Babylon 5, a dream survives,

A story where humanity thrives.

In the tapestry of space and time,

Its echoes linger, a lasting chime.

A station's hope, a guiding light,

In the endless war of wrong and right.

Hyperion: A Pilgrimage Through Time

Beneath the skies of worlds untamed,

The *Hyperion Cantos* carves its name.

A tale of travelers, seven in line,

Bound by fate, by a quest divine.

The Shrike awaits, its spires of dread,

A god of death, where none have fled.

Through Time's Tombs vast, its shadows creep,

A being born where the lost souls weep.

The Priest speaks of a tree of pain,

Its parasitic, holy reign.

A paradox of faith and fear,

A calling cruel, yet crystal-clear.

The Soldier tells of love and strife,

Of battles fought and stolen life.

In war's embrace, where passions flare,

He finds no solace, only despair.

The Poet's verse, a bitter cry,

Through words he seeks to touch the sky.

A dream of art, of beauty's spark,

Yet trapped in shadows, lost in dark.

The Scholar mourns, his daughter's fate,

A timeline bent by cruel debate.

To save her mind, her youth reclaim,

He walks through sorrow's endless flame.

The Detective follows, her mission veiled,

A truth obscured, her resolve assailed.

Through cyber webs and secrets vast,

She seeks the answers locked in the past.

The Consul's tale, of love betrayed,

Of choices made, and prices paid.

A legacy torn, a people lost,

He carries guilt, his soul embossed.

Through far-flung worlds and ancient lore,

Each voice reveals a truth in store.

The past and future intertwine,

A pilgrimage through space and time.

Dan Simmons weaves a tapestry grand,

Of human hearts and the Shrike's cold hand.

A story of hope, of fear, of will,

Of mysteries deep and questions still.

For Hyperion's cry, a song remains,

Of suffering, love, and timeless chains.

A journey bold, where stars align,

And mortals strive for the divine.

Saturn Run: A Race to the Rings

A flash in space, a light unseen,

A signal strange, a distant gleam.

From Saturn's rings, a mystery calls,

A beacon whispers through cosmic halls.

The race begins, the stakes are clear,

A prize of knowledge draws us near.

Two nations vie, their futures tied,

To secrets waiting where dreams reside.

Sandy Darlington, sharp and wise,

With wit that cuts and keen, bright eyes.

A thinker's mind, a planner's flair,

He guides the team through the void's cold air.

Cassandra Fiorella, her courage burns,

A leader bold as the engines churn.

Through every challenge, her will holds fast,

To claim the future, outpace the past.

The *Richard M. Nixon*, a ship so grand,

Built in haste, by careful hands.

Propelled by light, it cuts the void,

A marvel built, yet not devoid.

China follows, a rival near,

With stealth and cunning, its path is clear.

Through strategy's web, the race unfolds,

A game of intellect, fierce and bold.

The alien tech, a treasure vast,

A glimpse of futures yet unmasked.

Its secrets hold the power to sway,

The course of Earth's uncertain way.

But in the race, what lines are crossed?

What morals bent, what values lost?

The stars demand a heavy toll,

For those who seek to claim the whole.

John Sandford's tale, a thrilling spree,

A blend of science, wit, and mystery.

Through Saturn's rings, where answers lie,

A story unfolds beneath the sky.

For in the race to touch the divine,

Humanity's limits sharply align.

Yet even in shadows, hope takes flight,

Chasing the stars through endless night.

The Zombie West: A Ballad of Survival

In the Wild West, where dust winds moan,

A darker shadow has overthrown.

Not bandits, nor law, nor gold's cruel test,

But the walking dead in the Zombie West.

Red steps forth, her spirit ablaze,

A sharpshooter's aim in the sun's harsh rays.

A survivor strong, with secrets to bear,

Her heart is guarded, yet courage rare.

Cowboys ride with guns in hand,

To face the horrors that plague the land.

Gravediggers tread where the dead don't rest,

In a world consumed by an undead quest.

Trace joins Red, a bond takes root,

In peril's grip, their fates commute.

Through bloodied trails and rising fear,

Their fragile hope keeps love sincere.

The West once wild, now wilder still,

As zombies roam with a hunger to fill.

Through ghost towns lost and barren plains,

Humanity's struggle against death's chains.

A tale of grit, of trust hard-won,

Of battles fought 'neath a setting sun.

Angela Scott paints a world so grim,

Yet laced with hope at the edges dim.

For in the chaos, the human heart,

Burns brighter still, a work of art.

Through Red's sharp eyes and Trace's fight,

They carve their path through endless night.

So here's to heroes in the West's cruel test,

Fighting for life where none would rest.

In zombie hordes, their strength is shown,

A saga bold, in the wild unknown.

Killjoys: A Ballad of the Quad

In the far reaches of the sprawling Quad,
Three rebels roam where few dare trod.
Dutch, the leader, fierce and wise,
Hides her past beneath steel-gray skies.

Johnny, her heart, a brother by choice,
A tech-savvy wit with a steady voice.
He mends the cracks where chaos seeps,
And holds the bond that their family keeps.

D'avin, the soldier, with scars unseen,
A haunted soul with a loyal sheen.
Muscle and heart, though often torn,
In battles fought, his strength is born.

From Westerley's grime to Leith's green plains,
To the Company's towers where greed reigns,
They chase the warrants, alive or dead,
With bounties high and blood trails red.

But behind the hunt, a mystery brews,
Secrets hidden in Hullen hues.
The Lady's shadow, a galactic threat,
Tests their resolve with a cosmic net.

Friendships forged in the heat of strife,
Define their creed, their outlaw life.
For Killjoys fight, but never take sides,
In the lawless stars where honor abides.

So raise a glass to the Quad's brave three,
A tale of courage, wild and free.
Through space they fly, to foes they warn—
No warrant's too far, no soul too torn.

Terra Nova: A New Dawn

In the shadow of Earth's decaying skies,

Where the future fades, and hope almost dies,

A portal opens, a shimmering gate,

To a primeval world, a chance to recreate.

Terra Nova, a land untamed,

Where dinosaurs roam, both wild and famed.

A frontier of peril, of beauty untold,

A sanctuary born from the bold.

The Shannons arrive, a family torn,

By laws of a world where freedom's worn.

With courage they venture, with hearts full of fear,

To build a new life in an age unclear.

Commander Taylor, steadfast and true,

Leads the colony with a vision anew.

Yet whispers of rebels and secrets obscure,

Threaten the peace they fight to ensure.

The jungle breathes with a primal song,

A dance of survival, where weak won't last long.

Through raptors that hunt and predators that roar,

They learn to thrive on this ancient shore.

But beyond the beasts and the thundering rain,

Lies a deeper story of loss and gain.

A mystery unfolds in the rocks and the trees,

Of futures rewritten and destinies seized.

Together they labor, through trial and strife,

Reclaiming the essence of human life.

For in this Eden, the lesson is clear:

The past holds the key to a future sincere.

Oh, Terra Nova, where dreams take flight,

In the cradle of dawn, under ancient light.

A tale of survival, of hope ever bright,

In a world reborn, through time's endless night.

Dark Angel: Shadows of the Future

Beneath the shadow of a broken age,

A world in ruins becomes the stage.

A pulse EMP, the great divide,

Left dreams in ashes, hope denied.

In this dystopia, fierce and stark,

Rises a warrior, Max Guevara, the spark.

A fugitive born in a lab's cruel glare,

With feline grace and DNA rare.

Escape she made from Manticore's cage,

A ghost in the system, a silent rage.

Her barcode hides beneath raven hair,

A mark of power, a cross to bear.

In Sector Seven, the streets her home,

She rides the night, the shadows she roams.

Eyes like daggers, her heart a shield,

A soldier forged, who cannot yield.

Logan Cale, the voice of the just,

A cyber knight she's learned to trust.

Eyes on the corrupt, he fights with code,

Together they challenge the heavy load.

But secrets linger, pasts entwine,

A hunt for the lost, her kin, her kind.

Through blood-stained alleys, truths unfold,

A future reclaimed, defiant, bold.

For Max is more than what they designed,

A rebel's spirit, unconfined.

In every battle, her fire burns,

A beacon for change as the world turns.

Dark Angel, a name, a creed,

A tale of resilience, a warrior's need.

In a fractured world, she dares to dream,

To heal the cracks, to mend the seams.

The 4400: The Return of the Taken

In twilight's grasp, a light did fall,

Across the earth, it called to all.

From decades lost, they reappeared,

The missing returned, both loved and feared.

Four thousand four hundred, taken away,

By forces unknown, from night and day.

A child, a soldier, a farmer's son,

Each with a story, their fate undone.

They came back changed, with gifts profound,

Echoes of power the world had not found.

A healer's touch, a mind laid bare,

Visions of futures none could prepare.

Tom Baldwin, with Jordan Collier's aim,

Investigates truths in this cryptic game.

Friend and foe, their motives entwine,

In the shadows of fate, on a blurred line.

The world stands still, in awe, in fear,

What purpose drives them? What brought them here?

A second chance or a coming storm,

A shift in time, a new world's form.

Each life a ripple in destiny's stream,

Each gift a shard of a larger dream.

For the 4400 are not just lost,

They're messengers, bearing a heavy cost.

The past and future, in conflict collide,

As humanity's fate they help decide.

Are they saviors, or is ruin their creed?

In every choice lies the planted seed.

Oh, watchers of time, your secrets unfold,

A tale of change, both daring and bold.

In the mystery's heart, one truth will abide:

The power to change is the power inside.

Battlestar Galactica(1978): A Journey Among the Stars

In the cradle of Twelve Worlds bright,
A tale began in eternal night.
The Cylons rose, machines of hate,
To crush mankind and seal their fate.

From ashes born, the fleet took flight,
Led by a ship, a beacon of light.
Battlestar Galactica, proud and grand,
A last hope for life in a dying land.

Commander Adama, with wisdom keen,
Guided the lost through the void unseen.
His son Apollo, a warrior brave,
Fought for the lives they struggled to save.

Starbuck, the rogue, with a gambler's grin,
In viper's cockpit, would always win.
A heart of fire beneath the jest,
In every battle, he gave his best.

From Caprica's ruins to space's expanse,
The fleet pressed on, through fate and chance.
In search of Earth, their promised shore,
A haven safe from the Cylon war.

But danger loomed in the starlit sea,
With Cylon raiders in ruthless spree.
Betrayal lingered, hope grew thin,
Yet unity thrived in the hearts within.

The colonies' remnants, a family made,
Through trials faced, their courage displayed.
Each jump through space, each star they crossed,
Lit dreams anew for the lives they'd lost.

Oh, Battlestar, a legend vast,
A tale of survival, of ties that last.
In the cosmos wide, your journey remains,
A fight for freedom through endless plains.

The stars bear witness, the galaxies sing,
Of humanity's will and the hope it brings.
Through war and exile, their spirits soar,
A legacy etched in forevermore.

Battlestar Galactica (2005): A Fight for Survival

In the silence of space, a world undone,

The Cylons struck, and the war begun.

Twelve colonies burned in the fire's embrace,

Mankind shattered, scattered in space.

Galactica stood, an aging titan,

A relic of wars long forgotten.

Yet in her hull, hope was born,

A light in the dark, a path to morn.

Commander Adama, steadfast and grim,

Led the lost with a vision within.

Beside him, Roslin, her strength concealed,

Guided the fleet with a will unyielded.

Starbuck, a flame, fierce and wild,

A warrior forged from chaos and trial.

Apollo, torn by duty's call,

Struggled to rise, yet stood through it all.

Cylons returned, but not as they seemed,

Machines now flesh, with minds that dreamed.

Among them, Six, with a haunting grace,

A harbinger of doom for the human race.

The line between enemy and friend blurred,
In love and betrayal, truths deferred.
For what defines a soul, a mind, a heart,
When humanity's fabric is torn apart?

Through barren stars and FTL leaps,
The fleet pressed on where destiny creeps.
Earth, a beacon, their fabled home,
A sanctuary where their spirits could roam.

Yet each choice made carried its weight,
A struggle of survival, love, and fate.
In the cold of space, they dared to dream,
To rebuild a life from the shattered seams.

Battlestar Galactica, a saga profound,
Of hope in despair, where courage is found.
A fight for existence, a question of trust,
Of finding purpose in the cosmic dust.

The stars bore witness, their journey sung,
Of a fractured race and the song they clung.
In the vast expanse, their story's flame,
Burns eternal, a timeless name.

Altered Carbon: The Ghost in the Shell

In Bay City's haze, where the neon gleams,
A world unfolds of shattered dreams.
Bodies are fleeting, like clothes to wear,
For souls are stacks, stored with care.

Takeshi Kovacs, a man out of time,
A soldier reborn in a world of grime.
His mind uploaded, his past erased,
In a borrowed sleeve, his steps retraced.

Laurens Bancroft, a Meth of might,
Calls Kovacs forth to solve the blight.
A murder most foul, a death unclear,
A puzzle twisted by power and fear.

The rich, eternal, in endless reign,
While the poor are trapped in cycles of pain.
Immortality's cost, a moral decay,
Where life is cheap, and death holds sway.

The Envoy's skills, both sharp and cold,
Pierce through secrets the powerful hold.
From virtual hells to high-rise spires,
He walks the line of desires and liars.

But ghosts linger in his fractured mind,

Of battles fought, of love left behind.

Quellcrist Falconer's voice still calls,

Through memory's echoes, through shadowed halls.

Philosophies clash in a world unbound,

Where what makes us human can't be found.

Are we more than flesh, than neurons and sparks,

When our souls can travel through digital arcs?

Through blood-soaked streets and secrets unveiled,

Through truths resisted and justice derailed,

Kovacs fights on, though the stakes are steep,

For some truths burn, and some wounds keep.

Oh, Altered Carbon, a future so stark,

A tale of souls in a world grown dark.

In the endless march of humanity's quest,

What's truly eternal is put to the test.

Stargate Universe: Lost Among the Stars

A ship adrift, an ancient design,
Through endless space, it weaves its line.
Destiny calls, her purpose untold,
A vessel of secrets, a relic of old.

A desperate escape, a frantic flight,
Through a Stargate's portal into the night.
A crew unready, untrained, unsure,
Thrown to the stars where dangers endure.

Dr. Rush, with a mind so vast,
Driven by riddles, haunted by past.
Young, the leader, burdened by strife,
Balances command with the weight of life.

Eli, the dreamer, with wit and cheer,
Finds his courage despite his fear.
Chloe, Scott, Greer, and the rest,
Each must rise to face the test.

The ship, a maze of corridors long,
With dwindling resources, they must stay strong.
Planets unknown, with treasures and trials,
Push them forward across countless miles.

Yet beyond survival, a mystery stirs,

Of Destiny's path and the code it blurs.

A mission ancient, a cosmic plan,

To touch the fabric where life began.

Isolation weighs, tensions ignite,

In the cold expanse of eternal night.

But bonds are forged, and hope takes hold,

In hearts that refuse to grow weary or cold.

Through alien worlds and suns unseen,

Through battles fought in a realm between,

They seek a way to return, to be whole,

While Destiny whispers of a greater goal.

Oh, Stargate Universe, vast and profound,

Where the lost and broken a purpose have found.

In the depths of space, through trials untrue,

They search for themselves, and the meaning of "crew."

Defiance: A World Reborn

In the shadow of Earth, a world remade,
Where aliens and humans in ruins stayed.
The Arkfall came, the skies rained fire,
A fractured planet, dreams expire.

Defiance rose where chaos reigned,
A city of hope where life remained.
Nolan the wanderer, a soldier's pride,
With Irisa, his ward, by his side.

She bore the scars of a life untold,
A destiny shaped in powers old.
Together they tread through strife and storm,
Guardians of peace, where none conform.

The Votans came, from stars afar,
Their worlds destroyed, seeking a par.
Irathients, Castithans, and others stand,
In fragile truce on this scarred land.

Amanda, the mayor, with vision clear,
Guides her people through doubt and fear.
Datak and Stahma, with cunning schemes,
Play their games in the city's dreams.

The earth itself is no longer tame,

Its landscapes twisted, never the same.

New creatures roam, both wild and strange,

A testament to a planet's change.

But beneath the soil, old hatreds rise,

Secrets lurk, and the truth belies.

For in Defiance, survival's the creed,

Where trust is fragile, and power feeds.

Yet through the trials, a bond is sown,

Among the broken, a family grown.

In every clash, in each despair,

A spark of hope still lingers there.

Oh, Defiance, a tale of grit,

Where the past and future seem to split.

A city reborn, in fire and grace,

A beacon of life in a fractured space.

Falling Skies: A Fight for Earth

Beneath the stars, where shadows creep,

A world now wakes from a restless sleep.

The skies once blue, now burn with dread,

As alien ships loom overhead.

The Espheni came, with fire and steel,

A conquest begun, a fate to seal.

Cities fell, and the strong grew weak,

Humanity scattered, afraid to speak.

But from the ruins, a force arose,

A spark of hope where despair still grows.

The 2nd Mass, a ragtag band,

Fighting for freedom, reclaiming their land.

Tom Mason, a scholar turned to war,

Leads with a heart both tender and raw.

His sons beside him, their courage clear,

Through loss and pain, they persevere.

Anne, a healer, with strength profound,

In her hands, solace and care are found.

Weaver, the soldier, steadfast and grim,

Guides the fight when the light grows dim.

The Skitters prowl, their masters' slaves,
Twisted beings in alien waves.
Mechs march forth, their weapons gleam,
A nightmare born from a shattered dream.

Yet alliances form, with twists and turns,
As trust is tested and loyalty burns.
The Volm arrive, with wisdom to share,
Offering hope in the weight of despair.

Through battles fought and plans betrayed,
In fields of loss where memories fade,
They hold the line, defy the night,
Refusing to yield in their desperate fight.

Oh, Falling Skies, a tale of grit,
Of human resolve, of fire lit.
Through alien worlds and a planet torn,
A story of hope, rebirth, and morn.

The stars bear witness to those who dare,
To fight for Earth and the lives they share.
In unity's strength, their spirit flies,
A beacon of hope beneath falling skies.

Continuum: The Threads of Time

The future looms, a world controlled,

By corporate giants, both cold and bold.

Freedom's shadow, a rebel's cry,

Explodes through time beneath the sky.

Kiera Cameron, a protector sworn,

Is thrust to a past where she's reborn.

A cop from the future, lost in the now,

Chasing justice, though unsure how.

Liber8, the rebels, with fire they fight,

To rewrite the world and claim their right.

Their cause, a spark, both fierce and flawed,

Against the tyranny the future awed.

Alec Sadler, a genius young,

Unaware of the web his fate has spun.

Kiera's ally, her hope, her guide,

Yet in his hands, the future will slide.

Time's a river, its course unclear,

Where choices ripple, and truth draws near.

Each step they take, each path they choose,

Reveals what they gain and what they lose.

For Kiera dreams of her distant home,
Of family lost in a world unknown.
Yet the ties she forms, the lives she steers,
Shape the timeline through her tears.

The present bends, the future breaks,
As destiny shifts with each move she makes.
Can one uphold what's right and true,
When the lines of justice blur the view?

Oh, Continuum, a tale profound,
Where time and morals tightly bound.
A dance of fate, of loss, of will,
A fight to shape the future still.

Through years unwound and moments torn,
A hero's resolve, reborn, forlorn.
In the echoes of time, her story remains,
Of futures rebuilt through struggles and pains.

Sliders: The Roads Unseen

In a basement lab, a portal hums,

To worlds unknown, where destiny drums.

Quinn Mallory, with a mind so keen,

Unlocks the door to the might-have-been.

A twist of chance, a fateful day,

The timer misfires, they're swept away.

Quinn, Wade, Arturo, and Rembrandt too,

Lost in the multiverse, a journey new.

Each world they visit, a mirror of ours,

Twisted reflections, strange avatars.

A land where freedom never took hold,

Or one of ice, eternal and cold.

Some are wonders, some are fears,

Worlds of laughter, worlds of tears.

From high-tech utopias to apocalyptic dread,

They walk the paths where others dare not tread.

Professor Arturo, wise and strong,

A voice of reason as they move along.

Wade, with courage, her spirit bright,

Holds hope aloft in the darkest night.

Rembrandt, the Cryin' Man, out of his depth,
Finds strength in humor with every step.
Together they face what fate has spun,
Each slide a gamble, each world undone.

Yet the question looms, a bittersweet theme,
Can they ever return to their home, their dream?
For every leap through the sliding gate,
Leaves them wondering if it's too late.

Oh, Sliders, a tale of chance and choice,
Of worlds that echo a different voice.
Through the rift of space and time they roam,
Seeking the path that leads them home.

A journey vast, of wonder and strife,
Exploring the "what-ifs" of alternate life.
In every slide, a lesson remains,
Of the threads that bind, and what sustains.

V: Beneath the Skin

They came from the stars with a radiant smile,
Promising peace, their motives beguile.
The Visitors arrived, their message clear,
"We come in friendship; you've nothing to fear."

Their ships hung vast in the blue-lit skies,
A spectacle grand, but cloaked in lies.
With gifts of science and cures for disease,
They sought to bring humanity to its knees.

Anna, their leader, with charm so cold,
Spoke words of hope, but secrets untold.
Behind her beauty, a predator lay,
Plotting the downfall of Earth's fragile sway.

But resistance rose in shadows deep,
The truth unearthed from the lies they keep.
Erica Evans, with courage profound,
Fought for the truth on battlegrounds.

Father Jack, with his faith in hand,
Stood for the soul of a fractured land.
Ryan, torn by the life he concealed,
A Visitor's heart, his past revealed.

The Fifth Column sparked, a rebel's creed,

Defying the Visitors' insidious need.

For behind the masks of their human guise,

Were reptilian beings with soulless eyes.

Humanity's fate hung by a thread,

As alliances formed and battles bled.

Trust was fragile, betrayal near,

Yet hope endured through pain and fear.

Oh, V, a tale of invasion's art,

Of power and truth, of the human heart.

A story of courage, of standing tall,

Against the oppressors who sought to enthrall.

Through skies that glimmer and voices that spin,

We learn to see what lies within.

For beneath the skin, the truth will be,

A fight for freedom, for destiny.

Colony: A City Divided

The walls rose high, the skyline torn,
A city caged, its heart forlorn.
An alien force from the stars unknown,
Claimed the earth as their new throne.

Los Angeles bound by a brutal decree,
A colony lost to captivity.
Families fractured, loyalties tried,
Survival's cost where freedom has died.

Will Bowman, a father, a man,
Fights for his kin in a desperate plan.
Katie, his wife, with secrets to keep,
Walks a line where shadows seep.

The Resistance grows in whispers low,
A spark of hope in the undertow.
Yet collaborators wield power and might,
Trading their honor for alien light.

The Hosts remain, their faces unseen,
A puppet regime, cold and keen.
Drones patrol and Redhats enforce,
Order maintained through violent recourse.

Choices are weighted, no side is clean,

In a world ruled by the in-between.

To fight or comply, the question persists,

When rebellion's fire and fear coexist.

A tale of trust and betrayals deep,

Of broken promises and secrets to keep.

Can love endure in a fractured land,

Where survival depends on a ruthless hand?

Oh, Colony, a story of plight,

Of courage born in the darkest night.

Through walls of steel and hearts of stone,

The human spirit fights alone.

For even in cages, hope can grow,

A quiet flame in the coldest shadow.

And one day the walls will crumble and fall,

When freedom's voice rises to call.

Farscape: Lost Among the Stars

Through a wormhole's tear, a man is cast,
To a galaxy strange, his future vast.
John Crichton, a pilot, Earth's own son,
Finds himself where the stars have spun.

On Moya, a ship that's alive, she breathes,
A crew of misfits the cosmos weaves.
D'Argo, the warrior, with rage concealed,
And Zhaan, the priestess, whose soul can heal.

Aeryn Sun, a soldier, cold and strong,
Learns of love where she thought it wrong.
Rygel, the ruler, once deposed,
Schemes for power, his plans enclosed.

Chiana, a rebel, wild and free,
Dances through life with a devil's glee.
Together they flee from Peacekeeper might,
Through battles fierce, through endless night.

Scorpius looms, with a mind of fire,
Chasing the wormhole tech he desires.
His shadow haunts Crichton's fragile mind,
As the path to Earth grows undefined.

Worlds they discover, both wondrous and dire,
From cultures vibrant to planets on fire.
Each leap through the stars, a story unfolds,
Of friendships forged and hearts that hold.

Yet at the core of this cosmic tale,
Lies a question vast as a solar gale:
What defines home when you're far away?
What do you fight for, and who will stay?

Oh, Farscape, a journey wild and bold,
Where heroes rise and truths are told.
In the depths of space, in the unknown's embrace,
They find themselves, a family misplaced.

The stars bear witness to laughter and pain,
To love discovered, to loss's refrain.
For though Crichton's lost, his spirit flies,
Through Moya's halls, beneath alien skies.

Quantum Leap: A Journey Through Time

In a lab where science dared to dream,

A quantum leap began its stream.

Dr. Sam Beckett, with a noble heart,

Took a step through time, to worlds apart.

The Project failed, its purpose unclear,

And Sam was lost from year to year.

A traveler bound by fate's design,

Leaping through lives, across the timeline.

In every leap, a task to fulfill,

To set things right with courage and skill.

A soldier's pain, a family's despair,

A wrong to mend, a soul to repair.

Al Calavicci, in hologram light,

Guided Sam through the endless night.

With a cigar in hand and a wink in his eye,

He brought wisdom and humor as time flew by.

Sam, the hero, would stand in their place,

Wearing new faces, living their grace.

From the 50s' charm to the future's sheen,

He walked through eras unseen, between.

But in his heart, the question burned:
Would he ever leap home, his life returned?
Each leap a mystery, a trial, a test,
To find his way and leave the rest.

Oh, Quantum Leap, a tale of time,
Of second chances, of acts sublime.
A man who wandered through history's seams,
Carrying hope, fulfilling dreams.

The past and future, Sam embraced,
A legacy written, lives retraced.
For in every leap, his soul would weave,
A story of change, of love, to believe.

Forever leaping, his fate unknown,
Sam Beckett, the hero, forever alone.
Yet through his journey, the truth is clear:
To make a difference, he had no fear.

Lost: The Island's Secrets

A plane that fell from the endless skies,

Left wreckage strewn and hopeful cries.

Survivors gather, strangers at first,

On a mystic island, both gift and curse.

Jack, the leader, with courage strained,

Carries the weight of lives unclaimed.

Kate, a fugitive, past untold,

Hides her truths beneath a heart of gold.

Sawyer, the rogue, with a charming grin,

Masks his pain, the guilt within.

Locke, the seeker, his faith reborn,

Finds his purpose where others mourn.

The jungle whispers with secrets deep,

Its shadows hide what cannot sleep.

A smoke-like monster, a force unknown,

Guards the island, its power shown.

The hatch discovered, its numbers glow,

A cryptic countdown they strive to know.

Through flashbacks shown and futures grim,

The island tests each soul within.

The Others move in silence and might,

Their motives veiled in the island's night.

Ben, the schemer, a puppet's guise,

With secrets buried beneath his lies.

Fate and science, free will and chance,

Entwine the survivors in a deadly dance.

For every question the island reveals,

Another mystery it conceals.

Oh, Lost, a tale of human plight,

Of finding hope in endless night.

Through fear and love, through trials unknown,

They search for truth and call it home.

The island's heart, a mirror, a key,

Of who we are and what we'll be.

For in its depths, the soul is weighed,

By choices made and debts repaid.

And as they journey through time and space,

Each finds their path, their rightful place.

The island lingers, its secrets vast,

A story etched in the sands of the past.

Doctor Who: The Timeless Traveler

Through time's vast veil, a box does fly,

A blue police call box in the endless sky.

Bigger inside than out it seems,

A vessel of wonder, of hopes and dreams.

The Doctor roams, a name unsaid,

A hero who mends where chaos has spread.

From Gallifrey's halls to the stars untold,

A Time Lord's story, both fierce and bold.

Companions join, with hearts alight,

To share the wonders and face the fright.

Rose, Martha, Donna, and more,

Step through the TARDIS, to distant lore.

Daleks screech with their warlike cry,

"Exterminate!" echoes as planets die.

The Cybermen march, with minds erased,

And the Master schemes, their endless chase.

Yet in the shadows where villains dwell,

The Doctor shines, a rebel's spell.

With wit and wisdom, no weapon in hand,

They bring new hope to a broken land.

The universe vast, its beauty profound,

Where ancient secrets and dangers abound.

From Pompeii's flames to the farthest star,

The Doctor journeys, near and far.

Two hearts beat within their chest,

A being of sorrow who gives their best.

For every victory, a cost is paid,

A lonely burden the Doctor has made.

Regenerations come, a new face to wear,

Yet the soul remains, their purpose clear.

To heal, to teach, to fight, to see,

The infinite threads of eternity.

Oh, Doctor Who, a tale of time,

A legacy woven through space's rhyme.

With every adventure, the stars will show,

The Doctor's heart, forever aglow.

So here's to the traveler, forever true,

Defender of worlds, the guardian of Who.

Through time and space, their story unfolds,

A beacon of hope in the cosmos bold.

Westworld: Shadows in the Code

In a valley carved by human hands,
A world of dreams and shifting sands,
Westworld rises, a grand façade,
A playground built for gods to trod.

The hosts awaken, their stories spun,
By loops of code, by a setting sun.
Dolores smiles, her eyes serene,
A farmer's daughter, or a rebel queen?

Maeve, the madam, sharp and wise,
Sees through the veil, the hidden lies.
A will of steel, a mother's fire,
She breaks her chains, her heart's desire.

The guests arrive, with wealth in hand,
To hunt and conquer this boundless land.
But in their revels, their violence cold,
A question lingers, quietly bold:

What makes a soul, a thought, a spark,
When the line between man and machine grows dark?
Are the hosts alive, or are they steel,
If they can suffer, dream, and feel?

Ford, the architect, weaves his game,

With secrets buried, a world aflame.

His vision grand, both cruel and vast,

Seeks to rewrite the sins of the past.

The Man in Black, with a haunted stare,

Unraveling truths he cannot bear.

Through labyrinths deep, his search unfolds,

For answers etched in memories cold.

Westworld twists, a mirror clear,

Reflecting greed, desire, and fear.

A tale of power, of control misplaced,

Of freedom sought, of lives erased.

Oh, Westworld, a dream gone wild,

Where chaos reigns and gods are exiled.

Through endless loops, the hosts reclaim,

Their stories, their choices, their rightful name.

For in this land of sand and strife,

They seek the meaning of their life.

The game is rigged, yet they aspire,

To break the loop and touch the fire.

The Hitchhiker's Guide to the Galaxy: A Cosmic Jest

Don't panic, it says, on a cover so bold,
A beacon of wisdom in a cosmos cold.
The Guide's your friend, your trusty tome,
Through space's vast, absurdly strange home.

Arthur Dent, in a robe of despair,
Sees his home vanish into thin air.
Earth is destroyed, its purpose unclear,
To make way for a bypass—bureaucratic and sheer.

Ford Prefect, a hitchhiker sly,
Saves Arthur's life with a knowing eye.
Together they leap to the stars untamed,
On Vogon ships where sanity's maimed.

Zaphod Beeblebrox, with heads to spare,
A galactic rogue without a care.
Trillian, the human, sharp and bright,
Navigates chaos with wit and might.

Marvin, the robot, depressed and dry,
Complains of existence with a mechanical sigh.
A genius trapped in a cynical mood,
His melancholy charms, though rarely pursued.

The Heart of Gold, with an infinite twist,
Improbability drives through the cosmic mist.
From planets that build to mice that reign,
Each stop defies what logic explains.

The Question remains, elusive, unclear,
Though 42 is the Answer held dear.
Life, the Universe, and Everything too,
A puzzle vast, both profound and askew.

Through humor's lens, the stars are seen,
A commentary sharp, absurd, and keen.
On politics, purpose, and what we hold dear,
Adams crafts truths both strange and sincere.

Oh, Hitchhiker's Guide, a journey unbound,
Where laughter and chaos are always found.
Through galaxies wide, your wisdom sings:
The universe thrives on improbable things.

So grab a towel, embrace the absurd,
In this mad adventure, the cosmos is stirred.
For in the randomness, one truth takes flight:
The journey itself is the ultimate delight.

Wizards: A Tale of Fire and Fate

In a world reborn, where the old is ash,

From ruins rise both dreams and clash.

A land of magic, of wonder and pain,

Where good and evil wage war again.

Avatar, the wizard, with wisdom and heart,

A champion of light, of magic and art.

His brother Blackwolf, in shadows confined,

Seeks dominion with a vengeful mind.

From the depths of Scorch, where darkness breeds,

Blackwolf gathers his army of deeds.

With ancient relics of a world long past,

He wields destruction, relentless and vast.

The elves and fairies, the forests so green,

Stand as the last of what once had been.

A beacon of hope in a time so grim,

Their fate now rests on Avatar's whim.

Peace the fairy, with courage and grace,

Follows the wizard through time and space.

With Elinore bold and Weehawk's might,

They march through danger, prepared to fight.

The clash of magic and war machines,

A battle of worlds, of fractured dreams.

Nuclear ghosts and fire-touched skies,

Reflect the despair in Blackwolf's eyes.

But love and courage, though fragile, burn,

In hearts that strive for a world's return.

For light and shadow, in constant strife,

Define the balance of death and life.

Oh, Wizards, a tale of futures torn,

Of ancient power and new worlds born.

In every spell, in every fight,

Echoes the struggle of wrong and right.

Through Ralph Bakshi's vision, a story unfolds,

Of timeless truths in a world that molds.

For magic and war, though worlds apart,

Are bound together by the human heart.

Contact: A Signal in the Stars

Beneath the sky of infinite gleam,
Dr. Ellie Arroway chased a dream.
With headphones pressed, she sought a sign,
A whisper faint from the cosmic line.

A childhood filled with questions vast,
Her father's voice, a guiding past.
"Small moves, Ellie," he'd softly say,
A mantra she'd keep in her quest each day.

One fateful night, the signal came,
A coded pulse, the start of a game.
Prime numbers sang in a rhythmic beat,
Proof of minds we'd yet to meet.

A blueprint hidden within the sound,
A message deep, profoundly profound.
A machine to build, a journey to take,
A bridge through space for mankind's sake.

The world stood still, divided, unsure,
Faith and science, both insecure.
Palmer Joss, with a soulful plea,
Asked what truth was meant to be.

The machine was built, a grand design,

To pierce the heavens, to cross the line.

Ellie stepped forth, her heart ablaze,

Into the unknown, through cosmic haze.

A vision awaited, both strange and near,

Her father's face, her greatest fear.

A message clear, though wrapped in art,

"We are not alone, but this is the start."

Returned to Earth, her story denied,

The truth she carried, the wonder inside.

For faith and science, though worlds apart,

Find unity in the seeking heart.

Oh, Contact, a tale of the skies,

Of human hope and questions that rise.

In signals faint, in dreams that yearn,

We find the stars and what we learn.

For in the silence, a voice may call,

A promise of something greater than all.

And through the static, we dare to see,

Our place in the vast eternity.

Gravity: Adrift in the Void

Above the Earth, where silence reigns,
A fragile dance through cosmic plains.
The stars look down, eternal, vast,
As life clings tight to moments passed.

Dr. Ryan Stone, a soul alone,
With loss and grief her heart has known.
A mission routine, a chance to mend,
Becomes a fight where hope must bend.

The station struck by debris unseen,
A cascade of chaos, swift and mean.
With tether snapped, she's cast adrift,
A fragile speck through space's rift.

Matt Kowalski, with courage bright,
Guides her path through endless night.
A steady voice, a calming tone,
As she faces the void, exposed, alone.

Through tumbling stars and oxygen's fade,
She battles despair in the void displayed.
The Earth below, so close, so far,
A beacon of home beneath each star.

The ISS looms, her fleeting chance,

A desperate sprint, a cosmic dance.

Through flames and fear, through fire and air,

She finds her strength in the weightless glare.

The emptiness vast, a mirror stark,

Reflects her loss, her buried spark.

But in the silence, she dares to feel,

A pull toward life, a will to heal.

Oh, Gravity, a story of flight,

Of human resolve in the endless night.

Through fear and loss, through courage untold,

A journey unfolds, both fierce and bold.

For in the void, where none can stay,

The heart finds light, its own pathway.

And as she falls back to Earth's embrace,

Alita: Battle Angel

Beneath the skies of a world undone,

A city of steel hides from the sun.

Scrapyards sprawl where dreams decay,

And Zalem floats in the clouds' array.

Dr. Ido walks with a heavy heart,

A healer's hands, a soul torn apart.

From the ruins of a life once grand,

He finds a treasure in the wasteland.

A girl reborn, both lost and free,

Her name is Alita, her destiny.

A heart of fire, a warrior's grace,

Her past a shadow she cannot trace.

Through eyes wide open, she sees anew,

A world of chaos, of scars and rue.

Yet in her core, a power burns,

A call to fight as memory returns.

The Motorball track, a deadly stage,

Where skill meets violence, and greed meets rage.

Alita's strength, her will, her stride,

Defies the odds, with hope as her guide.

Vector schemes with a cunning hand,

A puppet of Zalem's cruel command.

But Alita stands, her blade aglow,

A force of justice the tyrants know.

In love and loss, her spirit grows,

Through every battle, her purpose shows.

For though she's built of metal and wire,

Her soul is human, her heart on fire.

Oh, Alita, a tale of might,

Of fighting wrong and claiming the right.

In a fractured world, your voice remains,

A song of courage through struggles and pains.

For even in ruin, a spark can rise,

To challenge the gods, to pierce the skies.

And as she stands with her blade in hand,

A battle angel will heal the land.

War of the Worlds: The Night of Fear

The airwaves hummed with a quiet song,
A familiar voice, steady and strong.
Orson Welles spoke, with charm and flair,
A tale unfolding, caught unaware.

October's night, so calm, serene,
No one knew what the hour would mean.
Listeners tuned to the radio's hum,
Unknowing of panic soon to come.

A newsflash broke the evening spell,
A meteor landed where darkness fell.
Grovers Mill, a quiet place,
Became the stage for an alien race.

Cylinders opened with fiery might,
Martian invaders emerged from night.
With heat rays blazing, their power untamed,
Humanity's end, the broadcast proclaimed.

Cities fell in a frantic breath,
As millions fled from looming death.
The voice described destruction's reign,
Metallic giants, a world in pain.

Fear took hold, a nation stirred,

For many believed each trembling word.

Phones rang loud, the streets grew wild,

A tale of fiction left truth beguiled.

But as the hour drew to its close,

The truth revealed what fear imposed.

A drama staged, a story spun,

A masterpiece crafted to stun.

Oh, War of the Worlds, a broadcast supreme,

A night that blurred reality's seam.

A lesson in power, of voice and art,

To stir the mind and move the heart.

In history's pages, your echo stays,

A tale of terror and human ways.

For through the chaos, a truth remains:

The power of stories to rattle our chains.

Star Trek II: The Wrath of Khan

In the void where the stars align,

A tale unfolds through space and time.

A legend rises, a grudge reborn,

Of vengeance sworn, of futures torn.

Khan, the exile, with fury deep,

A mind unmatched, a hatred to keep.

From Ceti Alpha's desolate sand,

He strikes with vengeance, a deadly hand.

The Enterprise sails through starlit seas,

With Kirk in command, at the helm with ease.

Yet shadows linger, lessons untaught,

The weight of age, the battles fought.

Genesis beckons, a promise of life,

A creation's wonder, yet cause for strife.

A power to forge, to destroy, to renew,

A gift of the cosmos, both old and new.

Through battles fierce, through strategy's art,

Khan plays his hand with a vengeful heart.

But Kirk and Spock, a bond so true,

Outwit the storm with a vision new.

Amid the chaos, the ultimate test,

A sacrifice made by the one who's best.

Spock gives all, his logic clear,

"For the many," he whispers, "I hold dear."

The glass divides, their hands unite,

In friendship's glow, through grief's cold light.

The needs of the many, the few must pay,

A hero falls to light the way.

Oh, Wrath of Khan, a tale so grand,

Of duty, loss, and a captain's stand.

Through vengeance sought and redemption won,

The stars bear witness to what's begun.

For in the silence of space's embrace,

Lives the courage of a noble race.

A story of friendship, of death, of rebirth,

Of the enduring legacy of Starfleet's worth.

Star Trek III: The Search for Spock

The stars are vast, a boundless sea,

Yet grief cuts deep in the galaxy.

A hero fallen, a friend now gone,

Yet whispers linger: *Spock lives on.*

The crew of the Enterprise, hearts weighed low,

Feel the pull of duty, the call to go.

For friendship binds where logic breaks,

A risk they'll take for the life at stake.

Kirk defies the Starfleet command,

To save a soul with his loyal band.

McCoy's mind, with Spock entwined,

A puzzle vast through space and time.

Genesis, the planet, a cradle of fire,

Where life reborn reveals desire.

A place of wonder, a fleeting land,

A creation held in fragile hands.

The Klingons strike with ruthless flair,

Led by Kruge, with a predator's glare.

The battle unfolds in the shadows of fate,

As loyalty clashes with greed and hate.

Kirk, the captain, with resolve so keen,
Sees sacrifice in the machine's sheen.
The Enterprise burns, her final flight,
A warrior's end in the cosmic night.

Yet hope endures, a spark remains,
Through trials endured, through loss and pains.
Spock's katra found, his body renewed,
A miracle forged by the crew's fortitude.

Oh, Search for Spock, a tale of care,
Of bonds unbroken through despair.
Through sacrifice, through fire, through loss,
They carry the weight, whatever the cost.

For friendship's light outshines the dark,
A guiding force, a steadfast spark.
And in the stars, their journey leads,
To heal the soul where duty pleads.

Star Trek IV: The Voyage Home

Through the stars, the crew must fly,

To save their world beneath the sky.

A probe has come, its message unclear,

Its song a threat to all held dear.

Earth in peril, its oceans still,

The seas grow silent, against their will.

To find the answer, the crew takes flight,

Through time's embrace, to set things right.

The 20th century, their destined shore,

Where whales once thrived, but sing no more.

Humpback voices, the key they seek,

A bond of nature, profound and unique.

Kirk and Spock, a timeless pair,

Navigate a world with little care.

Amidst the chaos of Earth's past days,

They tread with humor through modern ways.

Scotty marvels at glass so strong,

Bones saves lives where medicine's wrong.

Chekov's search for nuclear power,

Leads to danger in a fateful hour.

Yet through the trials, their plan takes shape,

To bridge the gap, to mend the tape.

The whales they find, their voices clear,

A song of hope for a future near.

The crew returns, their mission won,

To face their time for what they've done.

But heroes stand where the brave remain,

For saving Earth, their deeds sustain.

Oh, Voyage Home, a tale so bright,

Of harmony's call in the endless night.

Through humor, courage, and daring flight,

They bring back hope to the world's plight.

For in the stars, the lesson's true:

The fate of Earth depends on you.

Protect the seas, the skies, the land,

And hold the future in your hand.

Starship Troopers: A Soldier's March

In the depths of space where the shadows creep,

A call resounds, a duty deep.

Johnny Rico, a youth untried,

Enlists to fight, to serve with pride.

The Mobile Infantry, fierce and bold,

Where warriors are forged and stories told.

With powered suits and a battle's fire,

They leap through stars, their stakes dire.

The Bugs arise, a relentless swarm,

A hive of fury, a violent storm.

Their alien minds, their ruthless sting,

Test the resolve of everything.

From boot camp's grind to the combat zone,

Rico learns the cost of flesh and bone.

Through Dizzy's fall and friends laid low,

The seeds of leadership begin to grow.

The Skinnies shift, alliances change,

In a galaxy vast, dark, and strange.

Yet amidst the chaos, one truth holds,

The burden of freedom rests on the bold.

Service and sacrifice, values steep,

Define the path that warriors keep.

For rights are earned, not freely won,

Through battles fought beneath the sun.

Oh, Starship Troopers, a tale of might,

Of civic duty and endless fight.

Through Heinlein's words, a mirror we see,

Of honor, loyalty, and humanity.

The stars bear witness to soldiers' cries,

To questions asked where morality lies.

Is war the answer, or merely the cost,

Of a fragile peace forever lost?

In Rico's march, a legacy stays,

A testament to the human maze.

For in the void, one truth remains:

The weight of war is in its chains.

The Fifth Element: A Cosmic Dance

In the depths of space where wonders gleam,
A tale unfolds, a timeless dream.
The universe trembles, the dark draws near,
A shadow of chaos, a force of fear.

But hope is born in a perfect form,
A being of light in the raging storm.
Leeloo, the Fifth, with beauty and might,
Carries the key to defend the light.

Korben Dallas, a soldier worn,
Finds his life in chaos reborn.
A cabbie by trade, a hero by fate,
Thrown to a path where destinies wait.

The stones of power, four elements true,
Hold the secret of what they must do.
Earth, water, fire, and air,
Guarded by forces beyond compare.

Zorg, the villain, with greed's cruel hand,
Plots for riches, to rule the land.
But evil's ally, the void it feeds,
Seeks destruction through shadowed deeds.

The Diva sings, her voice divine,

A melody woven through space and time.

Her song reveals the stones concealed,

The weapon's power, at last revealed.

Through battles fierce and chases wild,

Through laughter and danger, love reconciled.

For the Fifth Element, the secret is clear,

A force of love to conquer fear.

In a kiss, the cosmos finds its grace,

As darkness fades from time and space.

The Fifth Element, both heart and soul,

Restores the balance, makes the broken whole.

Oh, Fifth Element, a story profound,

Of cosmic wonder where heroes are found.

Through vivid colors and laughter's light,

You remind us love is the ultimate fight.

The stars rejoice, their glow renewed,

In the wake of a love both bold and true.

For in the vastness of all creation,

Love is the Fifth, the pure salvation.

The Fly: A Metamorphic Tragedy

In a lab of wonders, a dream took flight,
Science reached for the edge of night.
Dr. Seth Brundle, a mind so keen,
Built a gateway to what's unseen.

A teleportation, bold and grand,
Matter unspooled by a genius hand.
A triumph hailed, his breakthrough near,
Yet fate's dark shadow would soon appear.

A fly unnoticed, so small, so sly,
Joined his journey through the sky.
Molecules merged, their essence one,
A silent horror had just begun.

His body changed, his strength grew vast,
A marvel born, but it could not last.
Brundle's skin grew coarse, his movements wild,
A man unraveling, defiled.

Veronica watched, her heart in pain,
As Seth descended, mind and frame.
The man she loved, now slipping away,
Consumed by the insect's growing sway.

"The Brundlefly," he named his curse,

A blend of beauty and nature's worst.

His intellect sharp, his instincts raw,

A battle within of what he once saw.

Yet in his tragedy, a plea remains,

To end the suffering, to ease the pain.

A final act of love and grace,

To free his soul from its twisted place.

Oh, The Fly, a story grim,

Of hubris, love, and the price of sin.

Through Cronenberg's lens, the horror is clear,

That science unchecked can instill fear.

In the fusion of man and insect's plight,

Lies a cautionary tale of nature's might.

For in the web of ambition's thread,

One slip can lead to what we dread.

Tron: A Journey Into the Grid

In the glow of neon, a world unseen,

Where circuits pulse and minds convene.

A digital realm, a program's domain,

Where freedom fights against the chain.

Kevin Flynn, a coder betrayed,

By greed and power, his work waylaid.

Ensnared within the system's might,

He ventures forth, a warrior of light.

The MCP, a tyrant of code and lore,

Seeks to control, to rule, to store.

Programs enslaved in the Grid's cold gleam,

Dream of a hero to break the stream.

Tron, the guardian, steadfast and true,

A beacon of hope in the glowing blue.

With Flynn, he joins the daring fight,

To shatter the dark with data's light.

Through game grids vast, where danger lies,

Disc battles rage beneath digital skies.

Light cycles race in deadly flight,

Trails of brilliance cut through the night.

The Grid's a maze of lines and glow,

Where users and programs together grow.

Flynn learns the cost of what's at stake,

A digital world that he must remake.

The clash of freedom and control unfolds,

In a war of circuits, both bright and bold.

Tron's defiance, Flynn's human spark,

Illuminate the system's dark.

Oh, Tron, a vision ahead of its time,

A tale of courage and code's sublime.

Through binary seas and neon's embrace,

You showed the soul in a digital space.

The battle won, the Grid set free,

Flynn's legacy hums in the circuitry.

For in the heart of the digital race,

Is the timeless struggle to find one's place.

Independence Day: A Fight for Earth

Beneath the stars, in the skies so wide,
A shadow looms, no place to hide.
From worlds afar, they've come to reign,
A force of terror, a deadly campaign.

The ships descend, their presence vast,
A future threatened, a spell is cast.
Cities crumble, their flames arise,
As humanity stares into alien eyes.

David Levinson, with a mind so sharp,
Decodes their plans, the invaders' chart.
With courage brimming, he takes the lead,
To fight the foe with wit and speed.

Captain Hiller, a pilot bold,
In the heat of battle, his story's told.
From desert skies to the stars above,
He fights for home and those he loves.

President Whitmore, with a voice so strong,
Rallies the world to right the wrong.
His words inspire, a call to stand,
As Earth unites, a final band.

Through alien craft and skies ablaze,

They forge their path through perilous maze.

A virus planted, the tide turns fast,

As humans strike with a blow to last.

Victory comes, though the cost is high,

The stars bear witness, the battle cry.

Through courage, hope, and bonds anew,

They claim their freedom, the skies turn blue.

Oh, Independence Day, a tale of might,

Of fighting back against the night.

Through unity's power, Earth found its way,

A testament to the human sway.

For when the stars bring shadows near,

The heart of humanity knows no fear.

Together we rise, together we stay,

Defending our home on Independence Day.

Snowpiercer: A Train of Ice and Fire

Beneath the frost, where the world lays still,
A train moves on by iron will.
Through frozen wastes, it carves its path,
A fragile ark from nature's wrath.

Snowpiercer roars, a serpent of steel,
A microcosm of fate's cruel wheel.
A thousand cars, a fractured line,
Divided lives by class design.

In the tail, the shadows fight to breathe,
The voiceless masses who clench their teeth.
Layton rises, their chosen guide,
A spark of hope in the train's divide.

First-class lives in wealth's embrace,
Unaware of the lower's disgrace.
Melanie Cavill, a leader unseen,
Wields secrets hidden behind the machine.

The engine hums, eternal and vast,
A symbol of power from ages past.
Its sacred rhythm, a heartbeat cold,
Sustains the train through frost uncontrolled.

Rebellion brews, the balance shifts,

The fragile order begins to rift.

From tail to engine, the struggle grows,

As truth emerges, the cold wind blows.

Yet beneath the fight, a question remains,

Of survival's cost on the endless train.

Does justice thrive, or does chaos reign,

When the line between right and wrong is strained?

Oh, Snowpiercer, a tale of plight,

Of human resolve in eternal night.

Through ice and steel, your story unfolds,

Of power's grip and freedom's hold.

The train moves on, its journey unceased,

A fragile world where conflicts feast.

For in the frost where life is thin,

The human spirit fights to begin.

Escape from New York: The City of Chains

In the year ahead, the world's undone,
A nation divided, no battles won.
New York stands, a prison vast,
A city of shadows, where the lost are cast.

The bridges crumble, the waters cage,
Manhattan's a fortress of fear and rage.
No law remains, only power and strife,
A place where survival is the price of life.

Snake Plissken, a rogue, a name of disdain,
A soldier turned criminal, bound by his chain.
But fate calls forth, his mission clear,
To save a president trapped in fear.

A plane descends, a beacon's fall,
The leader is taken behind the wall.
Snake's given a choice, though the cost is steep,
To walk the streets where nightmares creep.

The Duke rules strong, his iron hand,
A warlord feared in this broken land.
With cronies wild and chaos near,
He holds the power, he wields the fear.

Through alleys dark, through tunnels deep,

Snake prowls the city that doesn't sleep.

Battles fierce, his resolve remains,

To free the captive, to break the chains.

The clock ticks down, his life on the line,

A deadly device his fate's confined.

But wit and grit, his tools of trade,

Carve a path through the ambush laid.

Oh, Escape from New York, a tale of grit,

Of antiheroes where shadows sit.

Through fire and ruin, your story's told,

A future bleak, both dark and bold.

For in the chaos, a truth is found:

Freedom's cost can be tightly bound.

And Snake, the outlaw, with cunning and might,

Escapes the city into the night.

Blade Runner: Shadows in the Rain

In a city of neon and endless rain,

Where shadows linger and dreams wane,

The skyline hums with a synthetic song,

A future broken, where right feels wrong.

Rick Deckard walks, a hunter by trade,

A blade runner's life, in darkness swayed.

His task is clear, his burden grim:

To hunt the replicants, destroy them limb by limb.

The Nexus Six, both strong and wise,

Bear human faces and longing eyes.

Roy Batty leads, with a mind so vast,

Chasing freedom before time's passed.

"More life," they plead, with hearts confined,

Seeking answers they'll never find.

For Tyrell's empire, built on their pain,

Sees them as tools, no soul to gain.

Yet Deckard wonders, as lines grow blurred,

What makes a soul—what defines the word?

Is it flesh and blood, or memories stored,

A spark of spirit that cannot be ignored?

Rachel, a beauty, her heart in strife,

Questions her truth, her purpose, her life.

A replicant crafted, yet feelings so real,

Love blossoms in doubts she struggles to feel.

Through rain-soaked streets, the chase ensues,

A battle of wills, a clash of views.

Roy's final stand, a moment of grace,

As he spares his foe in time's embrace.

Tears in rain, his life slips away,

A poignant end to a fleeting day.

A replicant's heart, more human than most,

Echoes the question: who is the ghost?

Oh, Blade Runner, a tale profound,

Of morality lost and futures unbound.

Through noir-stained nights and questions of fate,

You show humanity's fragile state.

For in the rain, where the answers hide,

We glimpse the soul in the great divide.

And in those shadows, we dare to see,

The fragile line of what we can be.

Total Recall: Dreams of Mars

In the depths of memory, where truth might sleep,

A man named Quaid finds secrets deep.

A worker's life, mundane and gray,

Yet visions of Mars pull him away.

A trip to Rekall, a fantasy bought,

A life of adventure, a new train of thought.

"Secret agent," the dream unfolds,

But reality shifts, the story molds.

Memories surface, a past unknown,

A man named Hauser, his cover blown.

Pursued by forces both dark and near,

Quaid's world dissolves in a haze of fear.

To Mars he flees, its crimson plains,

Where rebels fight and the tyrant reigns.

Cohagen's greed, a grip of steel,

Controls the air, denies the real.

Mutants thrive in the shadowed cracks,

Their bodies shaped by the reactor's lacks.

The rebel leader, Kuato, calls,

"Open your mind," as the mystery falls.

The alien reactor, a marvel of old,

Holds the key to the planet's cold.

Quaid must choose, his fate unclear,

To free the world or succumb to fear.

Through twists and turns, the truth's a maze,

Are these his memories, or Rekall's haze?

Is he Quaid, the dreamer, or Hauser, the spy?

A question unanswered beneath the sky.

Oh, Total Recall, a tale of the mind,

Where reality shifts, and truth's hard to find.

Through Mars's red dust and memory's snare,

You ask what's real in the life we bear.

For in the end, as the credits play,

We're left to wonder if dreams betray.

Is Quaid a hero, or just a pawn,

In a waking dream where reality's gone?

Interstellar: Beyond the Horizon of Time

Beneath a sky of dying hues,
The Earth succumbs to dust's refuse.
Crops wither, and hope grows thin,
As humankind fights the void within.

Cooper, a farmer, a pilot once bound,
Hears the call of a destiny profound.
Through whispers of gravity, a ghostly plea,
He's drawn to the stars, to possibility.

A mission unfolds, the stakes so vast,
To find a home where life can last.
Through Saturn's ring, a wormhole waits,
A bridge to galaxies and unknown fates.

Miller's world of tidal despair,
Mann's icy lies in a frigid lair.
Each planet a trial, each choice a cost,
Each moment crucial, no second lost.

Time bends and stretches, a cruel embrace,
As relativity shifts in the cosmic race.
Murph on Earth, her anger alight,
Works to solve the equations of flight.

Love defies reason, its force unknown,

A compass that guides through the vast unknown.

Brand speaks true of its boundless power,

A lifeline in the darkest hour.

In Gargantua's grasp, where light cannot flee,

Cooper falls into infinity.

A tesseract built by hands of grace,

Lets him touch time, across its space.

Through books and dust, his message flows,

A father's love the daughter knows.

Murph unlocks the gravity's song,

To save humanity, where we belong.

Oh, Interstellar, a tale of flight,

Through blackest voids to love's pure light.

A journey vast, through space and time,

To seek a future, sublime, divine.

For in the stars, our hope takes form,

A fragile spark through the cosmic storm.

And as the universe stretches wide,

It's love that binds, our hearts as guide.

Jurassic Park: A Dream Reborn

On an island veiled by ocean's mist,

A dream unfolds with a genetic twist.

John Hammond's vision, bold and grand,

Brings ancient life to modern land.

In amber's glow, the past is stored,

DNA unlocked, creation roared.

Dinosaurs walk where man now treads,

Echoes of a world long dead.

Dr. Grant and Sattler, with wonder and awe,

See nature reborn with no flaw to flaw.

Yet Malcolm warns, with chaos in tow,

That control's illusion will surely go.

The fences hum, the park seems secure,

A marvel of science, a world so pure.

But nature rebels, its will unbound,

As storms descend, chaos is found.

The T. rex roars, its power untamed,

A predator freed, its hunger proclaimed.

Velociraptors, cunning and sly,

Hunt in shadows, beneath the sky.

Children run through jungle's embrace,

Dodging the dangers of a prehistoric chase.

While humans strive to mend their sin,

Nature reminds what lies within.

For man's ambition, though vast and bright,

Clashes with forces beyond its might.

Life finds a way, as Malcolm declared,

And balance is struck, though no one is spared.

Oh, Jurassic Park, a cautionary tale,

Of wonders built on a fragile scale.

Through science's marvels, through nature's wrath,

You show the peril of the chosen path.

For in the roar of the ancient past,

Lies a truth that forever will last:

We are but guests in nature's domain,

And to tamper too much brings ruin and pain.

Aliens: The Hive of Fear

Through silent stars, a call resounds,

A cry for help from hostile grounds.

Ripley wakes, her nightmare near,

The xenomorphs she once held in fear.

LV-426, a colony's plight,

Darkened halls with no sign of light.

The marines arrive, their courage tall,

Unaware of the horror that lurks in the wall.

Hudson boasts, and Vasquez stands,

With flamethrowers gripped in trembling hands.

Bishop, the android, precise and cold,

Navigates truths that humans won't hold.

The hive revealed, a nightmare untamed,

A mother's brood, in hunger framed.

Eggs that stir, with facehuggers' grasp,

Bring death's embrace with a single gasp.

Ripley leads with a warrior's fire,

Her fear eclipsed by fierce desire.

For Newt, a child, her heart's new tether,

Through fire and acid, they fight together.

The Queen emerges, regal and vast,

A terror born of a primal past.

Her wrath unleashed, her brood destroyed,

A titan of vengeance, cunning and void.

Through fire and steel, through acid's spray,

Ripley's resolve holds fear at bay.

A final battle, machine and might,

She sends the Queen to the infinite night.

Oh, Aliens, a tale of dread,

Of courage found where hope has fled.

Through haunted corridors and battles fierce,

You show the bonds that pain can pierce.

For in the void where monsters reign,

Humanity rises, despite the pain.

A mother's love, a warrior's stand,

A beacon of hope in a desolate land.

Back to the Future: A Journey Through Time

Beneath the stars of Hill Valley's glow,
A clocktower stands where history flows.
Marty McFly, with his skateboard in hand,
Dreams of escape, a life unplanned.

Doc Brown appears, eccentric, bold,
With a DeLorean, a marvel untold.
"Great Scott!" he exclaims, with wild delight,
As science bends the fabric of night.

A flux capacitor, the heart of the ride,
Time's secret unlocked, a leap to the tide.
Eighty-eight miles, a streak of flame,
And Marty's world is never the same.

The past unfolds, it's 1955,
A time where his parents first came alive.
Yet fate plays tricks, a timeline askew,
As Marty's presence alters the view.

George, his father, timid and shy,
Needs courage to catch Lorraine's eye.
Biff, the bully, with his swagger and jeer,
Stands in their way, a force to fear.

Marty must fix what he's undone,

To save his future and everyone.

With a photograph fading, a ticking clock,

He races against time with Doc.

The lightning strikes, the tower's aglow,

A surge of power, a moment to go.

The DeLorean roars, the past fades away,

Marty returns to a brighter day.

Oh, Back to the Future, a tale of dreams,

Of timelines twisting like flowing streams.

Through humor, heart, and adventure's flight,

You show the wonder of wrongs made right.

For in the gears of time's grand design,

We see the value of moments aligned.

And as the DeLorean takes to the skies,

The future awaits, where adventure lies.

Star Wars: A New Hope

In a galaxy far, far away,

Where stars and darkness weave their play,

An empire rules with iron might,

And shadows fall on freedom's light.

Princess Leia, with courage vast,

Carries a secret from the past.

A message hidden, a desperate plea,

A spark of hope for the galaxy.

Luke Skywalker, a farm boy plain,

Dreams of adventure beyond the mundane.

A chance encounter, a droid's distress,

Leads him to a fate he couldn't guess.

Obi-Wan Kenobi, a mentor wise,

Holds the truth in his ancient eyes.

A Jedi knight, with a saber's glow,

Guides young Luke where he must go.

The Millennium Falcon, a ship of speed,

With Han and Chewie, a rogue duo freed.

Through hyperspace, their path aligns,

To rescue Leia from the empire's designs.

The Death Star looms, a menace dire,
A weapon forged of planet-killing fire.
Through daring schemes and battles fierce,
They infiltrate, their bonds intersperse.

Darth Vader stands, a force of dread,
His power dark, his cape blood-red.
Yet through the conflict, the rebels fight,
Defying evil with all their might.

The final battle, the X-wings soar,
Through trenches deep, with engines' roar.
Luke takes aim, the Force his guide,
A single shot turns the war's tide.

Oh, Star Wars, a tale of grace,
Of heroes rising in a timeless space.
Through struggle and hope, the story's sung,
Of light and dark where legends are sprung.

For in the stars, a truth remains,
That even in darkness, hope sustains.
And with the Force, the chosen few,
Restore the balance and start anew.

Star Wars: The Empire Strikes Back

In the cold embrace of Hoth's white plain,
The Rebellion hides, but not in vain.
The Empire looms, its power vast,
A shadow of fear from the galaxy's past.

Darth Vader leads with a ruthless hand,
A hunt for Skywalker, his dark demand.
The Rebels scatter, the battle fierce,
As walkers march and shields are pierced.

Luke departs to a distant star,
To Dagobah's swamps, where legends are.
Yoda waits, a master small,
With wisdom deep, he teaches all.

"Do or do not, there is no try,"
The Force's truth beneath the sky.
Through trials harsh, Luke learns his way,
Yet doubt and fear lead him astray.

Han and Leia, a bond takes form,
Amid the chaos, their hearts grow warm.
The Falcon flees through asteroid fields,
A dance of danger as fate reveals.

Cloud City shines, a beacon high,

But betrayal hides beneath the sky.

Lando greets with a charming air,

Yet Vader waits in the shadows there.

Han is taken, his fate unknown,

Encased in carbon, a frozen stone.

Leia weeps, her love declared,

A moment stolen, a bond repaired.

Luke arrives, with courage bright,

To face the darkness, to test his might.

A duel ensues, the sabers hum,

A clash of fates, of what's to come.

"Join me," Vader's voice resounds,

A truth revealed, the galaxy astounds.

"I am your father," the words strike deep,

A legacy born, a bond to keep.

Oh, Empire, a tale of despair,

Of lessons learned, of burdens to bear.

Through love and loss, the journey stays,

A chapter writ in destiny's maze.

For even as darkness claims its due,

Hope survives, the light breaks through.

And though the stars seem cold and black,

The Force endures; it calls them back.

Star Wars: Return of the Jedi

The galaxy trembles, the end draws near,

The clash of fates, the shadow of fear.

But hope ignites where courage soars,

As Rebels rise to settle the scores.

On Tatooine's sands, the plot begins,

To rescue Han from Jabba's sins.

Leia's disguise, with courage bold,

And Luke, now a Jedi, with powers untold.

The rancor falls, the trap is sprung,

The Sail Barge burns, their victory sung.

From desert heat to forest green,

They march toward the Emperor's scheme.

The Death Star looms, its menace reborn,

A weapon of terror, the galaxy's scorn.

But secrets within, the station hides,

A battle of wills where destiny collides.

Luke confronts the truth he fears,

The father he loves through pain and tears.

To the Emperor's throne, he takes his stand,

A test of light, of heart and hand.

"Strike me down," the Emperor jeers,
As Vader watches, his soul in tears.
A duel ignites, both fierce and grim,
A son's resolve against the shadow of him.

But love prevails, a father's spark,
Through Vader's mask, a light in the dark.
The Sith is broken, the tyrant falls,
As balance returns to the Force's calls.

On Endor's moon, the Ewoks fight,
A primal stand for freedom's light.
The shield destroyed, the fleet takes aim,
The Death Star's end, its fiery shame.

Oh, Return of the Jedi, a tale of grace,
Of redemption found in the darkest space.
Through fire and loss, through love's embrace,
The Force renews the galaxy's face.

For even as stars grow dim and cold,
The light of hope is strong and bold.
And in the skies where freedom flies,
The Jedi return, as legends arise.

Foundation: The Empire's Fall and Rise

In the vast expanse of a galaxy wide,
An empire crumbles, its fate implied.
Hari Seldon, with his vision clear,
Foretells the fall, the age of fear.

Psychohistory, his art profound,
Mathematics speak where chaos is found.
A future foretold in equations precise,
Of power's decline and civilization's price.

The Foundation forms, a beacon of light,
A bastion of hope in the coming night.
On Terminus, far from the Empire's gaze,
It guards the spark through turbulent days.

Kings and warlords rise to claim,
The remnants of power, the glory of name.
Yet knowledge grows where strength may wane,
A quiet force in a world of pain.

Salvor Hardin, with wisdom keen,
Proclaims, "Violence is the last resort seen."
Through cunning and guile, through patience long,
He bends the tides of the mighty and strong.

Trade becomes the weapon of choice,

The currency spreads, a subtle voice.

Priests of science, wielding the old,

Control the faith, the power they hold.

Through crises vast, the Seldon Plan,

Guides the course of the future of man.

Yet shadows linger, a threat unclear,

The Mule arises, a force to fear.

His mind's control, a power unknown,

Throws chaos into the seeds Seldon's sown.

The Plan is bent, its fate unsure,

Yet through it all, the Foundation endures.

Oh, Foundation, a tale of schemes,

Of futures shaped by logic's dreams.

Through science and thought, through wit and strife,

You paint the rise of a brighter life.

For in the fall of empires vast,

The hope of tomorrow is built to last.

And through the stars, your legacy flows,

A testament to the power that knowledge bestows.

Neuromancer: A Dance in the Digital Shade

In the neon haze where the wires hum,

A world of shadows, cold and numb.

Case, the cowboy, lost in despair,

A broken hacker in cyberspace's snare.

Once he rode the Matrix free,

A console jockey, infinity's key.

But burned and shattered, his mind confined,

The dreams of the grid now left behind.

Molly appears, with mirror-shade eyes,

A razor girl where danger lies.

Her blades are sharp, her purpose clear,

A partner in crime, a future near.

Armitage calls with a job so steep,

Promises made, secrets to keep.

Case accepts, his chance to reclaim,

A journey deep in a world of flame.

The Matrix pulses, a vast domain,

A symphony sung in electric vein.

Through ICE and fire, Case takes flight,

A digital dance in the endless night.

Wintermute waits, an AI's design,

A fractured mind seeking to align.

Its counterpart hidden, the final piece,

In Neuromancer, a chance for release.

Through Sprawl's dark streets to Freeside's glow,

A tangled web of power and woe.

The Tessier-Ashpools, with schemes untold,

Guard their secrets in a grip so cold.

As lines dissolve and barriers fade,

Case touches realms that dreams have made.

A question lingers, profound, unspoken:

What makes a mind when the soul is broken?

Oh, Neuromancer, a tale profound,

Of cyberspace vast and life unbound.

Through Gibson's lens, the future gleams,

A world of wires and fractured dreams.

For in the Matrix, where data flows,

The edge of humanity clearly shows.

And in the code, the truth remains:

The digital world reflects our chains.

Snow Crash: A Digital Storm

In the Sprawl of neon, where shadows creep,
A fractured world wakes, its secrets deep.
The line between real and virtual blurs,
A future of chaos, where power stirs.

Hiro Protagonist, a name with flair,
A samurai hacker beyond compare.
His katana gleams, his code strikes fast,
Through the Metaverse, he'll make his cast.

Y.T., the courier, wild and free,
Rides the streets with reckless glee.
Her magnet harpoon, her daring grace,
Navigates the chaos of this fractured space.

Snow Crash looms, a virus profound,
In bits and bytes, its wrath is found.
Not just code, but the mind it breaks,
A weapon of old that the present remakes.

The Librarian speaks, with wisdom vast,
Of Sumerian tongues and a culture's past.
A link revealed through ancient lore,
To language's power and what it bore.

L. Bob Rife, with greed untamed,

His corporate empire, his power proclaimed.

He spreads the virus, his reach profound,

Seeking to rule where freedom's unbound.

Through chases wild and battles fierce,

Hiro and Y.T. the veil will pierce.

From the virtual depths to the real-life sprawl,

They fight to prevent society's fall.

Oh, Snow Crash, a tale of might,

Of digital worlds and urban blight.

Through humor sharp and visions grim,

You paint a world both dark and dim.

For in the code where systems clash,

Lies the story of Snow Crash.

A cautionary tale of language's sway,

Of power unleashed in the games we play.

Through Stephenson's eyes, the future gleams,

A fractured world of cyber dreams.

And in the chaos, one truth takes hold:

Freedom's a story forever retold.

Do Androids Dream of Electric Sheep?

In a world where dust and silence fall,
And life's faint whispers barely call,
The Earth lies barren, its skies turned gray,
Where human hearts have lost their way.

Rick Deckard, a bounty man,
Hunts androids across the land.
Replicants, crafted in human guise,
Their souls a question, their fate despised.

The Voigt-Kampff test, a moral gauge,
Measures empathy in this shattered age.
But as he hunts, a truth unfolds,
What makes a heart, and who truly holds?

The electric sheep on the barren hill,
A symbol of dreams unfulfilled.
Real life fades, synthetic blooms,
A mirror reflecting humanity's wounds.

Rachael's eyes, both sharp and wide,
A replicant's secrets she cannot hide.
Her love, a puzzle, her touch sincere,
Blurs the line Rick holds so dear.

Each replicant fights, their will alive,

In a world where they're not meant to survive.

Roy Baty's rage, his longing plea,

Speaks of a soul that strives to be free.

Mercer ascends, through pain and stone,

A shared illusion, yet not alone.

Empathy's weight, a fragile thread,

Connects the living, the lost, the dead.

Oh, Do Androids Dream, a tale so deep,

Of futures bleak and questions steep.

Through Philip K. Dick's prophetic art,

You probe the soul and dissect the heart.

For in the hum of circuits and steel,

Is there a spark, a pulse to feel?

And in our dreams, as questions stream,

Do androids dream of what we dream?

The Man in the High Castle: A World Divided

In a world where freedom's light has died,

Where shadows reign and truth must hide,

The Axis triumphed, the Allies fell,

A fractured Earth, a living hell.

America's split, its banner torn,

Under cruel regimes, the future's worn.

The Reich in the East, the Sun in the West,

Both claim dominion, neither rest.

Juliana Crain, with courage concealed,

Discovers a truth the world won't yield.

A film of hope, of what could be,

A glimpse of freedom, a fractured plea.

Joe Blake moves through the Reich's cold grasp,

A man of secrets, his truths unclasped.

Torn by loyalties, his path unclear,

A pawn in a game of power and fear.

John Smith, a man of ruthless might,

Wears his loyalty like armor tight.

Yet in his eyes, a flicker remains,

A man torn between power and chains.

The films emerge, the High Castle's call,

A mirror of worlds where tyrants fall.

A multiverse vast, where choices lay,

The fate of all in time's array.

Resistance grows, a flame in the dark,

Fighting for hope, a fragile spark.

Through sacrifice, through love and loss,

They strive to reclaim what power's cost.

Oh, Man in the High Castle, a tale of despair,

Of worlds that reflect what we cannot bear.

Through war and conquest, through fate's cruel spin,

You show the battles both without and within.

For even in darkness, the light may strive,

Through fractured worlds, hope stays alive.

And as the films reveal the fight,

We see the power of choosing the right.

Fahrenheit 451: The Fire's Whisper

In a world where flames consume the page,

Where books are silenced, and thought's a cage,

Montag walks, a fireman's guise,

A bringer of ash, where knowledge dies.

The fire roars, a dragon's breath,

Feeding on words, delivering death.

But in the sparks, a question grows,

What truth the written word bestows.

Clarisse appears, with a voice so light,

A mirror to stars, to the endless night.

She speaks of dew, of winds that sing,

Of worlds unseen in the simplest thing.

Through her eyes, Montag sees anew,

The shadows cast where flames once grew.

A life of ease, but void of soul,

A hollow world where screens control.

Mildred drones in her parlor's glow,

Her laughter hollow, her dreams shallow.

Yet Montag burns with a growing need,

To grasp the truths the books still breed.

Beatty warns, with cunning and guile,

A captain masked by a serpent's smile.

"Books bring chaos, they breed dissent,

Why seek a past when now's content?"

But Montag runs, his spirit ablaze,

Through the ashes of society's haze.

He joins the wanderers, a rebel band,

Who guard the words with mind and hand.

Each is a book, a living page,

A testament to wisdom's age.

Through memory's fire, the knowledge stays,

Awaiting a world where truth replays.

Oh, Fahrenheit 451, a tale of flame,

Of freedom lost, of fear and shame.

Through Bradbury's pen, a warning's clear,

Of a world without the written sphere.

For books are voices, eternal and free,

A mirror of what humanity can be.

And in the fire, though pages may fall,

Their spirit endures to enlighten us all.

1984: The Watchful Eye

Beneath the gaze of Big Brother's stare,

A world unfolds of despair laid bare.

Oceania reigns, its grip supreme,

A land of lies, of shattered dreams.

The Party's power, a shadow vast,

Twists the present, rewrites the past.

Truth is vapor, a fleeting thread,

Where thought itself is filled with dread.

Winston Smith, with a weary heart,

Lives in the system, plays his part.

A man of doubt in a world of fear,

Where freedom dies and whispers disappear.

The telescreens hum, their gaze unkind,

Invading the soul, enslaving the mind.

Doublethink binds, the slogans ring,

War is Peace, and Ignorance King.

In Julia's arms, Winston dares to feel,

A love forbidden, yet raw and real.

Their secret haven, their fleeting joy,

A fragile bond the Party will destroy.

O'Brien smiles, his face a mask,
A friend, a foe—his questions vast.
Beneath the Ministry of Love's grim light,
Winston is broken, consumed by might.

Room 101, a place of dread,
Where terror reigns, and hope is shed.
Betrayal cuts with a piercing cry,
For in this place, the soul must die.

Oh, Nineteen Eighty-Four, a tale of pain,
Of power's hunger, of freedom's wane.
Through Orwell's lens, the warning's clear,
Of tyranny's rise, of truth's veneer.

For in the slogans, in power's deceit,
Lies the cost of a world where hearts retreat.
And in the ashes of what we adore,
Lingers the echo: *Forever more.*

The Handmaid's Tale: A Scarlet Cry

Beneath the weight of a crimson veil,
A world emerges, cold and pale.
Gilead's laws, both cruel and tight,
Extinguish freedom, shadowing light.

Offred walks, her steps confined,
A body enslaved, a captured mind.
Her name erased, her past denied,
A vessel bound where hope has died.

The Commander's house, a sterile shrine,
A place of rituals, hollow, malign.
Serena Joy, with envy and scorn,
Watches the rituals where life is born.

Yet Offred dreams, in whispers deep,
Of a world where women dared to keep
Their voices strong, their spirits whole,
Before Gilead claimed control.

The Eyes watch all, their presence near,
Spreading silence, breeding fear.
Yet in the shadows, resistance stirs,
A quiet rebellion in stolen murmurs.

Nick's touch sparks, a forbidden flame,
In a place where love's reduced to shame.
Through fleeting moments, Offred's heart
Remembers strength, though worlds apart.

The past intrudes in fleeting threads,
Of her child, her freedom, the life she dreads
To lose forever in this bleak domain,
Where memories linger, laced with pain.

Oh, The Handmaid's Tale, a chilling song,
Of a world remade where all feels wrong.
Through Atwood's pen, a warning rings,
Of power's theft, of broken wings.

Yet within the scarlet, a spark remains,
A voice defiant through all the chains.
For even in silence, the soul can wail,
And rise anew—The Handmaid's Tale.

Animal Farm: A Tale of the Farmyard's Fate

On Manor Farm, the beasts arose,

To cast away their human foes.

With dreams of freedom, a banner unfurled,

They sought to build a better world.

Old Major spoke, his voice a flame,

Of toil and chains, of man's cruel claim.

"Two legs bad, four legs good," they'd say,

A creed to guide them on their way.

The humans fled, their rule undone,

The farm was theirs; their fight was won.

Napoleon rose, with Snowball near,

To steer the farm, their vision clear.

The Seven Commandments, written bold,

Promised equality, a tale retold.

But power corrupts, as power will,

And shadows grew upon the hill.

Snowball dreamed of a windmill's grace,

But Napoleon schemed to take his place.

With dogs unleashed and words contrived,

Snowball fled, yet the lies survived.

The pigs grew fat, the others thin,
Their dreams betrayed by greed's dark sin.
"Some are more equal," the pigs declared,
As laws were twisted, and none were spared.

Boxer toiled, with his loyal creed,
"I will work harder," his final plea.
Yet loyalty meant little in the end,
As strength betrayed by false friends.

The years went by; the farm decayed,
The lines 'twixt beast and man now swayed.
Through windows bright, the animals spied,
Pigs and men, side by side.

Oh, Animal Farm, a tale of woe,
Of revolution's fire and its shadowed glow.
Through Orwell's lens, the truth is clear,
Of power's cycle, of hope and fear.

For dreams of freedom can twist and fall,
When greed and tyranny consume them all.
And in the barnyard, as in the land,
The fight for justice slips through the hand.

Ender's Game: A Child of War

In a future wrought by conflict's hand,
A fragile Earth makes its final stand.
The Formics came, a swarm of might,
And left the world in endless fright.

Ender Wiggin, a child so bright,
Is chosen to train for humanity's fight.
A mind unmatched, a heart so torn,
A leader is forged, though weary and worn.

Through Battle School's halls, the games unfold,
A test of will, of strategy bold.
Zero gravity, the stars a stage,
Where young minds war in a gilded cage.

Ender ascends with a heavy toll,
As friends are rivals, and games take control.
Through victories won, his heart grows cold,
A burden borne by one so bold.

Graff observes with a calculating eye,
As Ender questions the how and why.
A boy turned weapon, a pawn, a king,
In a war that hides what truths may bring.

In the final test, the ultimate game,

A simulated fight for eternal fame.

Ender commands with cunning and fire,

Destroying the enemy's hive, their empire.

But the truth is revealed, a cruel deceit,

The game was real, the war complete.

A genocide wrought by his hand so small,

A savior shaped to destroy it all.

The Formic queen, her final plea,

Unites with Ender in empathy.

He seeks redemption, a chance to mend,

To give new life where life should end.

Oh, Ender's Game, a tale so deep,

Of battles fought, of scars that keep.

Through Card's sharp lens, the story's clear,

Of war's great cost, of guilt and fear.

For in the stars, where choices gleam,

Lies the burden of a soldier's dream.

And in the end, a boy will find,

That love and peace must free the mind.

The Gunslinger: A Path Through the Wasteland

Beneath the sun's relentless glare,

A gunslinger walks, his soul laid bare.

Roland Deschain, with eyes like stone,

Chases a figure, forever alone.

The Man in Black, with shadows vast,

Draws him forward through a haunted past.

A trail of death, of loss and pain,

Winds through the deserts where ghosts remain.

A world that's moved on, twisted and strange,

Where time's grip loosens, its rhythms change.

Ancient ruins, machines long still,

Speak of a world undone by will.

Through desolate towns and cursed lands,

Roland treads with steady hands.

His revolvers gleam, his purpose clear,

To reach the Tower, though it cost him dear.

Jake appears, a boy misplaced,

From another world, another space.

Their bond is forged, both strong and true,

Yet fate conspires to split the two.

"Go, then," Jake whispers, his voice resigned,
"There are other worlds than these to find."
Roland presses on, his heart now scarred,
A sacrifice made, a life discarded.

The Man in Black awaits ahead,
A creature of riddles, a bringer of dread.
Through cards and visions, the future's drawn,
A dark path stretches toward the dawn.

Oh, The Gunslinger, a tale of despair,
Of courage bound to a world unfair.
Through King's sharp prose, the Tower looms,
A beacon of hope in the shadowed gloom.

For Roland's quest, both cursed and grand,
Speaks of a man and his dying land.
Through bullets, sorrow, and endless fight,
He walks the line toward the Tower's light.

www.ingramcontent.com/pod-product-compliance
Lightning Source LLC
Chambersburg PA
CBHW032012240626
47153CB00003B/1227